Joshua and the Shadow of Death

Book 1
The Berserker Series

Copyright © 2018 by Gary McPherson
Charlotte, North Carolina

All rights reserved. No parts of this book may be used or reproduced by any means, graphic, electronic, or mechanical, including photocopying, recording, taping, or by any information storage retrieval system, without the written permission of the publisher except in the case of brief quotations embodied in critical articles and reviews.

This novel is a work of fiction. Names, characters, places, and incidents are either products of the author's imagination or used fictitiously. All characters are fictional, and any similarity to people living or dead is purely coincidental.

Cover design and interior by Ebook Launch

First, to my wife, a woman who believes in me even when I do not.

Second, to "The Creative Way."

Third, to the team of people who have helped me with my first novel.

Finally, to my readers. Thank you for buying, reading, and telling others about this book and the books to come. Without you, I could not afford to share my stories.

You can find my website here:
https://gmacwriter.com

Prologue

Malibu, California

1999

"Dr. Zeev, won't you please call the orphanage? Harry keeps pleading for us to bring his brother home."

Psychiatrist Joshua Zeev looked down at his blank computer screen. The black glass reflected the shadow of a man who felt older than his forty years. *Why did I agree to come all the way to California? This child doesn't have separation anxiety, hyperactivity, or even berserker syndrome. He's demonic.*

Joshua sighed and stared at Barbara again, unsure of what to say. Her long, thick black hair shone in the sunlight streaming through his office window. Her fair complexion, large blue eyes, and ideal skin gave her the appearance of a living doll. Joshua wondered why such a beautiful couple would agree to adopt and raise such a troubled child.

"Dr. Zeev, what are you thinking?" Barbara asked.

Joshua sighed and leaned back in his chair. "Please, like I've said many times before, call me Joshua. That's what I prefer my friends call me."

Barbara smiled and nodded.

Joshua continued, "I was thinking about how good it will be to hear Dr. Adam's North Carolina accent again."

Barbara reached across the desk and grabbed his hands. "So you are going to ask for us?"

Joshua nodded. "I will talk to Adam and see what we can do, but don't get your hopes up. You know we haven't heard from Harry's mother since she dropped off Bill and Harry at the orphanage. She was a very disturbed young lady. You can't imagine the hell she went through when her uncle raped her, and then, to have his child. You shouldn't be surprised Harry has the troubles he has, given how he came into this world."

Barbara let go of Joshua's hands. "Yes, but at least she did decide to have him. She could've tried to have some back-alley abortion. I can't say I would've blamed her. It sends shivers down my spine every time I think of her going through that nightmare. It's even worse because she was just a child despite what her body showed."

Joshua sighed and slightly pushed back his desk chair. He turned toward the window that looked across the street. It was all part of Richard and Barbara's estate. Joshua often thought the lot across the road had the best view and would go wander around up there when he needed to think. However, he knew abruptly ending their meeting so he could go think would be rude, so he attempted to hide away in his mind for a moment.

"What is it, Joshua?" Barbara asked in a soft voice.

Joshua smiled to himself and kept staring out the window. "Oh," he said, "just a memory. A good memory. When I met Harry's mother, April, she was a mess, but she wanted to get better. And for a while, she was. I had her on medication to deal with anxiety and depression, and she would make regular visits to see Harry in the baby ward at the orphanage. Eventually, she was able to take him back."

Joshua's smile left him, and he turned to face Barbara. "I'm not sure what set her back down her dark path. I wish I had fought her for custody of Harry's brother, Bill, but I didn't. I thought she would come back to get Bill like she promised. Allowing her to maintain custody and leave Bill at the orphanage seemed logical back then. But now, I doubt Bill will ever see the outside of the orphanage grounds until the day he becomes an adult."

Barbara asked, "Why did she do that? It just seems cruel to me."

"I would like to say she was being altruistic, but in truth, she was only thinking of herself. Harry was a symbol of the innocence she had stolen from her, and so she wanted nothing to do with him. I'm just thankful she brought him back to the orphanage instead of dropping him in a gutter somewhere. By the time she gave away custody, she hated everything about Harry." But Bill—April adored that child. She said Bill was everything his brother wasn't. Bill was the seed of her love with another man."

"But what happened to that man?" asked Barbara.

Joshua stretched his arms over his head and then relaxed, resting his hands on his desk. "He was around, but April wanted nothing to do with him. I don't know if she had quit taking her medication or what happened, but in the end, she developed multiple personalities. The dominant personality wanted nothing to do with this man she claimed to adore. It was that new personality that convinced April that if she left Bill at the orphanage, she could return one day to get him when her mind was settled. So April never gave up custody, and we have yet to hear from or see her."

Barbara took out a tissue and wiped a tear trailing down her cheek. "That poor woman. Those poor boys. It's no wonder our Harry is so disturbed. Do you think the state will release Bill to us?"

Joshua frowned. "Honestly, I doubt it. You are here in California, and Bill is in North Carolina. The last address April lived in was in North Carolina. I don't think the state will want us sending her child all the way across the country. There is nothing about his life at the orphanage that's cruel. To be honest, after my work with him, he became a well-adjusted young man. I'm sure he would prefer a family, but the courts will not remove a child and give custody to a non-family member simply because his biological mother has not shown up yet. If you attempt to push this too far, the courts could decide he should no longer be in the orphanage and may put Bill into a foster home or with relatives he doesn't know. I will talk to Adam, but I suggest you don't hold out much hope."

Barbara's eyes were glassy, and she nodded her head. "I just want to help Harold deal with his loneliness and do what we can for his brother."

Joshua took her hand. "You and Richard are doing all you can, and I'm here. If I didn't think we could help Harry, I wouldn't have left the orphanage. All those boys were my children, but I could see how much you and Richard loved Harry. It will take time but have faith."

A howl echoed down the large Spanish estate's hallway. The lonely cry reverberated like the call of a wounded coyote and transformed into a deep guttural growl. Barbara and Joshua leaped from their chairs and nearly ran over each other as they made their way down the hallway to the far end of the house.

They passed by the foyer and then the entrance to the kitchen before suddenly stopping in their tracks. Richard lay wounded on the hallway floor. Blood trickled from his head and stained the Spanish tile. A five-foot-tall child appeared from the doorway to the left, his breaths heavy and quick. Sweat dripped from his thickly curled red locks, and spittle flew from his lips. He had a large book lifted over his head, ready to strike Richard.

Barbara screamed, "Harry! Stop!"

The child looked up at Barbara and Joshua with rage in his bloodshot eyes. "My name is Harold!" he roared in a voice far too mature for such a young man.

Joshua took a step forward and put his hand up. "Harry, you will take the book back to your room and wait for me."

As if a switch had flipped, the boy slowly lowered the book as he turned back toward his room. He stopped for a moment and looked back at Joshua and his mother. This time when he spoke, his voice sounded more like a ten-year-old child.

"Joshua, will you take me to our special place?"

After Joshua nodded, Harold dropped his head and went skulking into his room.

Joshua walked over and examined Richard's head before helping him to his feet. He could see his new friend was upset. "Don't worry, Richard. I will talk to Harry. It's going to take time."

"Why doesn't he want us calling him Harry, Joshua? Why are you the only one who can do that?"

Joshua shrugged. "I honestly don't know. I assume it's because I have worked with both him and his brother. It could be that he doesn't want to be called Harry by either of you because you are his new life, his forever family, and he doesn't want you reminding him of the orphanage."

"But you remind him of the orphanage," Barbara interjected.

"I know. My advice is to call him Harold. That is the name he connects with being your son. I don't know why it matters so much to him. So far, he has refused to share his naming preferences with me."

Blood began to drip down Richard's face. Richard pulled a handkerchief from his back pocket and wiped away the blood. Joshua put out his hand, and Richard gave him the cloth.

Joshua applied pressure to Richard's fresh wound. "Why don't the two of you let me deal with Harry? Barbara, please attend to this wound and put a bandage on Richard's head. Thankfully, it's only superficial."

Richard held the cloth to his head, and Barbara slipped her arms around him. "I hope he didn't hurt you too badly with that book."

Richard gave a half-hearted smile. "It looks like the pen can be mightier than the sword."

Joshua squeezed his shoulder. "Especially if you're unarmed."

Barbara and Richard walked back toward the other side of the estate to their master bedroom. Joshua took a deep breath and turned his attention to Harold.

Joshua walked into Harold's room. The boy sat on his large double bed with his legs hanging over the edge. Although large for a child his age, Harold sometimes resembled the two-year-old child Joshua remembered from the orphanage.

All the books had been tossed about the stucco-colored room, except for one. On his walnut desk sat the C.S. Lewis book *The Lion, the Witch and the Wardrobe*. Joshua could see that Harold had begun reading it a short time ago.

As he sat down at Harold's desk, Joshua turned toward the bed. Harold's eyes were calm, and tears streamed down from the face of a boy truly sorry for what he had just done.

Joshua decided he would start. "Harry, I have a question for you. Why do you want me to call you Harry instead of Harold?"

Harold shrugged. "I don't know. It's the name I remember from the orphanage. I don't really remember anything else."

"Then why do you get mad when your mom and dad use that name?"

Harold looked at his hands and rubbed his fingers together while he spoke. "I just like Harold. It sounds more grown up. Harold Brown. The name Harry, and you, remind me of my past and my brother. Harold reminds me of who I am now and who I hope to be when I'm grown up. Your question is boring. This place is boring. When are we going to take our trip? You promised me we would go there to talk."

Joshua pulled out his pen. "I want you to focus on my pen."

Harold rolled his eyes. "I already know all of this, Joshua."

"You're a smart young man," Joshua said as he lowered the pen, "but you need to follow my directions."

Harold nodded, and Joshua raised his pen again. Joshua spoke calmly and quietly in an almost monotone voice. His rhythmic speech purposefully maintained a slow, steady beat. Soon Harold's eyes drooped down.

"Harry, where are you?"

"I'm in our ringed fortress."

"That's right. We are in the village near the gate. Tell me what you see."

"The trees are green, and the land is covered in heather."

Joshua stood up and walked over near Harold. "Let's walk to the longhouse."

"Okay," Harold said in an excited voice.

The child slid off his bed and followed Joshua down the hall to his parents' bedroom. Barbara and Richard were not there, but Joshua heard them in Richard's office at the end of the hall. Harold and Joshua strolled into Richard's office. Barbara and Richard were behind his desk. She had just finished patching his head. Both looked surprised to see Joshua standing in the room with Harold.

Joshua put his finger to his lips, lowered it, and then spoke. "Okay, Harry. We're in the longhouse.

I believe you have something to say to your parents, the King and Queen Trelleborg."

Harold lowered himself to one knee and bowed his head. "I'm sorry, Mother and Father. A son should never attack his parents. Do whatever punishment seems fit."

Barbara caught her breath and covered her mouth. Tears filled Richard's eyes. Joshua simply nodded their way.

Richard spoke up. "You are forgiven, Harold. There is no punishment if you allow us to teach you how to control your anger."

"It would be my honor," said Harold, still looking at the floor.

"You may go," Richard said as he wiped the tears from his cheeks.

Harold stood up, and Joshua spoke, "Harry, let's take a walk to the village wall and talk."

Harold nodded and gave Joshua a distant look. The two walked from the office, down the hall, and into the Southwestern-decorated living room. Harold followed Joshua around the overstuffed tan couches draped with serapes and through the French doors that led to the sundeck of the home. The two walked out and sat at a table. Joshua took a deep breath. The salty cool air from the Pacific Ocean that glistened in the distance helped to relax his stressed body. He looked over at Harold, who seemed to imitate him.

"What do you see, Harry?"

"I see our kingdom. Our fields, the woods, and our happy subjects, but I don't see my brother."

Joshua took Harold's hand. "I'm afraid Bill can't come live with you. He must serve in his own kingdom."

Harold scowled. "You mean he's a prisoner to that awful witch."

Joshua sighed, remaining quiet for a moment while he thought of a response. "Yes, Harry, he is her prisoner, but only for a little while. You can't blame your parents for her actions. Your parents are powerful, but even they can't free Bill from a faraway kingdom."

Harold bowed his boyish head. "I know. I'm sorry."

Joshua knew it was time to stop. "Harry, it's time to leave, but you will remember everything we have talked about."

Harold's face looked disappointed, and he sighed but nodded. Joshua slowly brought him out of the kingdom he had traveled to in his mind. Harold's eyes lost their glassy, distant look.

"How are you feeling?" Joshua asked.

Harold smiled. "Better, thanks. I wasn't expecting to end up outside."

Joshua shrugged. "Well, I like the warm California sunshine, and look at this view. Besides, I may want to go swimming in the pool when we're done."

"But you have your clothes on," Harold said.

"You are an observant young man."

"Joshua, can we walk down by the pool and talk a little more? You know, here, not in the place you built in my mind."

Harold's suddenly mature request surprised him. "Sure."

Joshua led the way down the concrete steps that rested on the side of the hill to the infinity pool that sat on the edge of a level hilltop. Joshua stopped at the pool's edge and admired the view of the homes nestled in the mountains below them.

From behind, Harold's voice yelled, "What's up, Doc!"

A hard shove propelled Joshua forward before he knew what hit him. His instincts took over, and he put out his foot to stop his fall. Unfortunately, the only thing to rest his shoe on was the pool's water. Joshua plunged into the eighty-degree water of the heated pool. At the pool's edge, Harold stood pointing and laughing. Soon he was doubled over from laughing so hard at his own joke.

Once the shock wore off, Joshua also started laughing, not only about Harold's joke but also for joy. It was the first practical joke Harold had played on him. The two had now grown close enough that Harold felt comfortable pulling a prank. Joshua reached down to his pocket, relieved to find his flip phone missing. Joshua slowly made his way to the pool's edge in his waterlogged clothes.

He raised his hand toward Harold. "Help an older man up, young man."

Harold grabbed Joshua's right wrist with both hands. Joshua effortlessly tossed Harold over his shoulder and into the pool before Harold had time to react. The boy came up sputtering and laughing.

He splashed water toward the doctor and shouted, "Hey, Doc! That's not fair!"

Joshua feigned indignity. "That's Dr. Zeev to you, young man."

Harold swam over and grabbed the edge where Joshua floated. He shook his head and water slung in every direction.

He looked at Joshua with his face beaming. "Nope, from now on you're just plain Doc to me. It's gonna be Doc this and Doc that for as long as we are friends. Now I have a dad and a doc."

Joshua laughed and nodded. "Okay, Harry, you win this round. We should probably go in and get cleaned up before your mother catches us in her pool with our clothes on."

Just then the back door opened, and both the doctor and the boy froze. Joshua let out a sigh of relief when he saw the young housekeeper, Maria, coming out with towels and her index finger on her lips.

Joshua forced himself to ignore her tan skin, her long, straight, shiny hair that fell to her waist, and her small proportional frame. He had been attracted to her since the first day he arrived in California. Unfortunately, he knew nothing would ever come of the two of them. Maria was in her late twenties, more than ten years his junior, and Harold was more than he could handle for the foreseeable future.

Maria quickly made her way down to the pool as Harold and Joshua finished getting out. "Please, hurry," she said in a hushed conspiratorial tone. "My mother was watching you both and sent me. She is keeping Barbara in her bedroom with silly questions, but you must hurry."

Harold took off toward the house, doing his best to dry, walk, and run all at the same time. Maria stayed behind with Joshua.

"Thank you, Maria. You're a lifesaver."

Joshua leaned down and gave Maria a kiss on her soft, cool cheek. Maria blushed and turned away.

"Please, señor," said Maria, "you must go too."

Joshua nodded and started up the hill, but instead of going to the back door, he diverted his path to the gate at the left of the estate. Peeking around it, he made his way to the garage and his car.

"What are you doing?"

Joshua jumped at the sound of Maria's voice.

He whispered, "Where did you come from? I didn't hear you following me."

Maria giggled and then whispered back, "I can be sneaky when I need to be."

Joshua took out his key and unlocked the car. He knew Maria would cover for him, so he said in a hushed tone, "I can't go to my room. It's right across from Richard and Barbara's bedroom. Tell them I am going to the gym."

"But where are you going, señor?" asked Maria.

"To the gym. I have my bag in the back of my car. I can shower and change clothes there. I'll be back in half an hour."

Maria giggled again and went into the house through the garage entrance. Joshua backed out of the driveway, laughing as he drove down the winding mountain road. His day had not gone as planned. Joshua navigated down the two-lane road with his heart full of pride. He knew he was making headway with the family. Everything would be better, but it was going to take time.

Joshua pulled into the parking lot of the Malibu Plaza. He grabbed his gym bag out of the trunk and entered the gym. He pried out his membership card from his soaked wallet. Although his clothes were no longer dripping, he had clearly been submerged in water shortly before arriving.

The woman at the entrance looked at his card and said, "A little pre-workout swim before the real thing?"

Joshua chuckled. "Something like that. A friend of mine decided I needed some time in his pool before coming in. I promise I'll dry out before getting on the equipment."

The young lady smiled, and Joshua went into the locker room. The warm shower felt good on his chilled body. He slipped into his workout clothes and decided to spend a few minutes on an exercise bike. From that vantage point, he could get in a light workout and enjoy the view of the beach across the street. Joshua dug around his gym bag and was thankful to find his flip phone where he last left it. He headed onto the deck to start his short workout.

Keeping a slow but steady pace, Joshua opened his phone and dialed Adam's number.

"North Carolina Children's Home," came the sound of a familiar voice.

"Dr. Adam, how is my old friend?"

"I'm doing good. To what do I owe the pleasure of your phone call?"

"I was just missing an old friend and the Piedmont," Joshua responded.

He heard Adam laugh on the other end.

"Really? Tell me, Dr. Zeev, what are you looking at right at this moment?"

Joshua was quiet before replying, "A beach in Malibu and the Pacific Ocean."

"Bless your heart. Y'all really suffer out there. I'll be praying God will strengthen you in your time of suffering."

Joshua's laughed and lost his rhythm on the exercise bike. He stopped himself and restarted.

"What is that hum I keep hearing, and why do you sound like you're breathing harder?" asked Adam.

"Um, I'm at the gym."

Adam's voice dripped with sarcasm, "When will your suffering ever stop? I honestly don't know why you're not running back to North Carolina. How can you stand the strain?"

Both men laughed.

Dr. Adam continued, "Seriously, Joshua, what can I do for you?"

Joshua stopped peddling and looked around the deck. He was alone.

"Richard and Barbara are still pushing to adopt Bill. I told them I would call."

Adam's voice took on a serious tone. "I thought you and I agreed that we would never pursue that. You know Bill could end up in foster care—or worse, with one of April's relatives."

Joshua nodded to himself as he held the phone to his ear. "We did, and we won't. I promised them I would call and ask, and I have. I'm going to tell them you said there isn't a way to make it happen. This way nobody is lying."

"You always were the smart one, Joshua."

"How is Bill doing these days?"

Adam's voice softened. "He misses you. All the boys here miss you. Bill was so young when Harold was adopted, he doesn't remember his brother. I've told him you were called away to help a family friend with their child. There is no reason to cause Bill the additional trauma of knowing you are with a brother he doesn't remember."

"Has Bill regressed any?"

"No," said Adam. "He is the same model child you left. I still don't understand how you turned off his switch. It seems like just yesterday he broke a boy's arm and was flipping over picnic tables at the age of five."

Joshua looked around to confirm he was still alone. There was nobody on the deck except a lone sea gull that had stopped on the guardrail at the far end.

Joshua replied, "I can't say I have a formula. That's part of the reason I wanted to work with his brother. Bill responded quickly to the hypnotherapy. We dealt with his rage in a simulated battle and in conversations around imaginary campfires. Harold is much too violent to try the former. I have only been able to deal with him after he goes berserk. I put his mind in a quiet location and help him understand the damage he has caused. I don't know if I will ever be able to get him to the stage I got Bill."

"Do you think there is something genetic involved?" Adam asked. "After all, Harold is a child of incest. Maybe there's a recessive trait or mutation we don't understand that is affecting his mind."

"Possibly," said Joshua, "but I'm not sure why Bill would exhibit the same symptoms, just to a different degree, if it was genetic."

"If you figure that out, Dr. Zeev, you'll be on the front page of the *New England Journal of Medicine*."

"I'd settle for a solution without any pomp and circumstance."

"And that's why I think of you as my protégé and a friend."

Joshua smiled, and then the men said their goodbyes. He went back inside and got his gym bag full of wet clothes. Joshua drove with the window rolled down and soaked in the mild California weather on his return to the estate. He was surprised to see Maria step out into the garage as he pulled his car in. She walked to the back of the car and waited for him to open his trunk. As soon as the trunk popped, she reached in and grabbed the gym bag.

Joshua quickly climbed out of the car. "You don't have to do that. I'll wash those."

Maria shook her head once. "No, this is my job. You need to take care of Harold."

"Did something happen while I was gone?" Joshua asked with concern.

"No," said Maria. "He is working on his homework in his room, but you have your notes to do."

Joshua was intrigued Maria knew what he did. "You're very observant."

Maria blushed and said, "I watch everything you do. Now please, get to work. Mr. Richard and Ms. Barbara are counting on you."

Joshua nodded and headed toward the garage door. He knew the family was relying on him. He just hoped he could solve their problem.

Chapter 1

Malibu, California

2017

Joshua sat slightly bent in front of his computer, his eyes deeply focused on the monitor. The ache in his back tried to distract him, but he pushed it aside. His momentary discomfort did not concern him, only the burden of his work. He plucked away at the keyboard, ignoring the world around him. For eighteen years, he worked with Harold to bring his rage under control. Joshua could scarcely believe time had flown by so quickly. When he first arrived, Harold had been a young boy of ten years old, and Joshua a forty-year-old man at the peak of his career.

Joshua paused for a moment, raised his arms, and stretched his back. He once more pondered his success with Harold's brother Bill.

Joshua worked with Bill's rage issues at the orphanage until he was eight years old. By that time, Bill showed no signs of the rage Joshua had defined as the berserker syndrome. He had named it after April and her Danish heritage. Much like her sons, the berserkers were known to fly into an uncontrollable rage. Christian warriors who faced them in battle had often accused the men of being possessed by demons. The berserkers were known to wear animal skins and seemed immune to attacks by steel or fire while they were in their rages. Some old stories told of them swallowing live coals, biting into swords, and obtaining supernatural strength and fighting abilities. Their fierceness on the battlefield was so feared that even their own people would fall back to avoid the wrath of a berserker.

Unfortunately, the treatment that worked with Bill did not benefit Harold. Joshua shook his head in frustration while he thought about his work over the years. Harold had all the advantages, including loving, wealthy parents who adopted him and brought him to California. Joshua admired and respected Richard and Barbara Brown. The couple always puts others before themselves and Harold above everybody else.

Richard ran his defense company inside the lines. He believed in caring for his family first and his employees second. He said on several occasions that if you take care of people, they will take care of you. The success of Parabolic Defense Systems testified to and validated his vision. Barbara stood as the rock and foundation of the family. She was everything a boy could dream of in a mother. Barbara's love for Harold had known no end during his difficult teen years. Even Joshua had trouble liking Harold during that time, but Barbara's love for Harold as a teenager was beyond his expertise. After Harold had turned sixteen, Joshua argued to have him hospitalized, but Richard and Barbara would not hear of it. So Joshua remained with the family, determined to give such brave and loving parents his full support.

Joshua knew Harold's ongoing condition could not be a byproduct of his upbringing. He resumed the update of his records in frustration. *I have worked with the patient for eighteen years trying to solve the berserker syndrome. Over time, Harold's rage and superhuman strength have become more controlled, but they have never gone away. His half-sibling seemed to overcome this condition before puberty and never again exhibited it. The only significant difference between Bill and Harold is that Harold is the result of an incestuous rape. I wonder if there is a genetic anomaly involved?*

Joshua sat back and sighed. *What am I missing?*

A loud pop went off down the hall toward Richard's office, but his own thoughts consumed him. Then a howl vibrated the walls of the hallway. Joshua's closed office door rattled inside its frame. He immediately knew something was horribly wrong. Joshua lunged for the doorknob and swung the door open. He sprinted out the door toward Richard's office and found the door open. Through the opened door he could hear a woman crying and the smashing of furniture. Joshua held up his pace just short of the door. Peeking through, he found Barbara cowering on the floor. Harold's large hands gripped a massive oak bookshelf over his head. He threw it with one mighty heave against the wall. The shelf embedded into the wall and splintered. Joshua quickly grabbed Barbara and pulled her from the room.

She buried herself into Joshua's chest and sobbed. "He shot himself! Why, Joshua, why?"

Joshua attempted to calm Barbara's trembling body. "Who shot himself? Harold?"

"No! Richard. Richard killed himself! Why?"

Joshua stood there holding Barbara. His mind went numb at her words. Inside the office, he could hear Harold's deafening cries of rage and anguish. He didn't dare go in to check on Richard until Harold stopped going berserk. He held Barbara to restrain her from going to Harold, as well as to comfort her.

Barbara attempted to wiggle free of Joshua's grip. "I need to go to Harold."

Joshua strengthened his arms around Barbara's struggling body. "Not right now. Let him calm down. Your son will be okay soon."

The sound of shattering glass and breaking wood eventually ceased. Joshua heard footsteps and looked up. All six feet, five inches of Harold stood in front of him. His thick red locks clung to his forehead in sweaty curls. Tears flowed from his piercing blue eyes. His father's blood stained his shirt and hands and part of his tearstained face. In his arms, he held his father's limp body. Blood still oozed from the opening in the back of Richard's skull. Barbara screamed and fainted in Joshua's arms. Harold stared at Joshua with a look of deep sadness and pain.

Pointing to the door on his left, Joshua said, "Harold. Please. Put your father in the guest room there. I need to tend to your mother."

His world was spinning, but Joshua knew he needed to focus. Barbara's heavy body lay unconscious in his arms.

Harold's grunts emanated from the bedroom, and the bed squeaked with the weight of Richard's lifeless body. Joshua gently knelt and eased Barbara to the floor. He fanned her face and stroked her cheek until she woke up.

Barbara looked up at Joshua. "Please help Harold. Don't let my son hurt himself or us."

Joshua nodded and helped her sit up against the hallway wall. He could hear Harold crying as he got up and looked into the bedroom. Harold bowed over his father's lifeless body, weeping. Blood made a macabre halo around Richard's head on the pillow. Harold still looked more like a monster than a man for the moment. Joshua decided it was best to give Harold solitude to process his grief.

Taking a deep breath, Joshua walked into Richard's office. Richard's desk and chair had survived Harold's onslaught. The rest of the furniture sat splintered, and glass shards from the curio cabinet lay splayed all over the floor. Pieces of statues and awards stuck into the hardwood, and bits of everything penetrated the textured tan walls.

Joshua choked back his tears and tried to remain as dispassionate as possible. His best friend lay dead in the other room, and the wall behind his desk held bits of his brain and blood.

Why would he do this? Why didn't I recognize the signs?

Guilt and doubt screamed with grief inside Joshua's head. He noticed the gun lying on the floor. Thankfully, it had gone unnoticed by Harold. Joshua picked it up, unloaded the remaining bullets, and dropped them in his pocket. He quickly put the gun back in the desk drawer and locked it. A freshly folded piece of paper sat under an old dusty ashtray. He pulled the bloodstained paper out. Richard's neat handwriting spelled out his despair and love.

My dearest Barbara, Harold, and my good friend Joshua,

I am so sorry. I have failed you. I have failed so many friends. Our company has been targeted by people I thought were our friends. These men are in the process of taking everything from us: our company, our home, everything we hold dear. How can I possibly protect you all when I can't tell my enemies from my friends? Their attack on me is targeted not only at the business but my personal life with all of you. Perhaps my death will stop these men or slow them down until Harold can find a solution. This is the only way I know to protect you all. Joshua, keep my computer. There may be evidence on it that you and Harold can use to save our company and family. Maybe in this way, my death will serve some purpose. I love you all dearly.

Joshua, I'm sorry I could not come to you. Even you can't save a man whose reputation is about to be falsely ruined.

Love,
Richard

Joshua squeezed the paper inside his fist and walked backed to Barbara. He stuck out his fist, and she carefully slid the note out of his hand. Barbara read Richard's desperate words and began to sob. They heard Harold's heavy footsteps, and both held their breaths. His massive frame emerged from the guest bedroom. Joshua could see some calmness restored in his eyes.

"Harry, your father left a letter."

Harold walked over, slid down the wall next to his mother, and read the note. They held one another and sobbed. Joshua stepped away to his office and wept. *He couldn't come to me? Why? He killed himself so people wouldn't talk behind his back? What was wrong? Richard, my friend, I think you just ended both of us.* Joshua could not stop the self-pity that seemed to be taking over this mind.

After few minutes, he composed himself. Joshua peeked down the hall and saw Barbara's small five-foot-four frame cradling Harold's head. She looked like a child cradling a giant. He walked back to his desk, drew in a deep breath, and dialed 911.

"This is Dr. Joshua Zeev at the Brown residence. We need the police and EMTs. Richard Brown has shot himself in the head."

"I'm sorry. Did you say there was a shooting?"

"Yes, a suicide. Richard Brown shot himself. Please get people over here quickly."

Joshua hung up. The California sun streamed into the office from the window behind him. He sat down on his old blue couch. It was a favorite furniture piece he had brought with him from North Carolina, and it looked so out of place amidst the stucco, tans, and browns inside his office at the Spanish-style estate.

He thought of the first time Richard pleaded with him to come to California to treat their son. They sat on the couch in his office at the orphanage. Joshua had sat where he sat now. Richard and Barbara had left Harold in California with John Richmond and his family for two days so they could make the trip. At the time, Joshua was convinced he would solve Harold's condition in two years—or possibly three years, at most. Wiping fresh tears from his cheeks, Joshua drew in a deep breath to garner his courage. He rose and walked out to Harold and Barbara.

Joshua squeezed Harold's shoulder. "I think we should go outside until the authorities arrive."

"I'm not leaving my dad!"

Joshua did not want to agitate Harold. He spoke softly and slowly. "He's gone now. Let's go outside so we can be out of the way. Your mother can call my cell phone if she needs us." Joshua reached over and touched Barbara's shoulder. "Why don't you wait in the foyer till the police arrive?"

Harold sat up and looked beside him at his mother. She slowly nodded in agreement. He stood and overshadowed Joshua by half a foot. His shoulders left little room between the walls. Harold led the way, and Joshua took Barbara by the hand and followed him to the foyer. Barbara crumpled into the nearest chair. Maria peered around the edge of the doorway at the three of them.

Joshua tried to give a gentle smile. "Maria, it's okay. You may come in."

Their housekeeper burst into the foyer and straight into Barbara's arms. The two women wept.

Joshua could see Harold's strained look and knew it was time to get him outside. He opened the door, and a warm breeze gently blew onto the group of mourners there in the foyer. The two men walked out into the blinding sunlight. Joshua closed the door on the darkness behind them.

The beautiful Southern California sunshine brought a momentary relief to the shadows behind the front door. They walked the short distance across the small atrium to the turquoise entry gate. Both men stopped at the driveway. Neither one knew which direction to go. Joshua considered his options. Should they walk over to his home across the street or go and sit on the pool deck?

"Why don't we walk around to the back and sit by the pool?"

"Okay, Doc," Harold replied softly before sniffling.

The two walked in silence. They followed the narrow white gravel path that dropped away from the concrete driveway. Both men stopped at the pool deck overlooking the rolling brown Malibu hills and the sparkling Pacific Ocean below. Joshua loved this part of the home. For eighteen years, he had wandered to this spot daily. It never seemed to get old, only more inspirational. Today his numbness masked the beauty. He sat at the round table next to the pool. Pulling a chair closer to his, he invited Harold to sit down close to him. Harold complied and stared out over the ocean. Neither man spoke or even looked at the other. The breeze wafted the sounds of the town from below. Time stood still for Joshua. He could taste the slight tinge of sea salt in every breath. The pump on the infinity pool hummed in the background. He jumped when Harold quickly buried his large head into his shoulder.

Harold began to sob again, and Joshua tried to comfort him. "Your father was a good man, a strong man. He just made the wrong decision. I'm sure he thought it was going to help somehow. If he had known how badly this would hurt you and your mother, he would probably still be alive. None of us imagined he would ever do something like this."

Joshua's dark thoughts shamed him with his own statement. *You should have imagined. It's who you are, or who you thought you were.*

Joshua's shirt stuck to him, soaked with Harold's tears and Richard's blood, but Harold showed no signs of slowing down. He felt relieved Harold's rage had diminished, but his heart broke for his young friend. He needed to keep Harold as calm as possible. Harold's violent tendencies always surfaced when he felt cornered. Then he became a different man, a man capable of ripping apart all the patio furniture and Joshua along with it. Grief and sadness would fill Harold's upcoming days. Joshua would have his work cut out for him. *I still don't understand his condition. How can I possibly help him deal with this?*

Richard trusted Joshua to take care of his son. *He must have trusted me. Richard would never abandon Harold. Richard couldn't come to you. Why would he trust his family to you?* Joshua tried to push away the evil condemnation filling his mind, but he knew he was losing the battle.

The howl of dogs rose eerily up the hillside, announcing the oncoming police and EMTs. Joshua knew he needed to get to the house but only if he could keep Harold from coming with him. Harold witnessed his father shooting himself in the head, and his temper hung by a thread. Peace and quiet were what Harold needed most.

Joshua raised Harold's head from his shoulder. "Would you mind waiting here while I go help your mother?"

Wiping tears from his face, Harold nodded. Joshua walked back to the house and opened the rear French doors to the living room.

By the time he left Harold and entered the room, the police had arrived, and a flurry of activity had already started. The sour smell of death brought Joshua back to the horror just out of sight down the hall. A man in a polyester navy blue suit with striped tie and a police identification badge hanging off the front pocket walked up to him.

"Who are you, sir?"

Joshua stared intently at the man's ID badge. "Detective Rodriguez, is that correct?"

"Yes, sir, and you are …?"

"My name is Dr. Joshua Zeev. I live in the ranch home across the street."

Detective Rodriguez began to write in his small notebook. "Oh, yeah. That smaller house with the big porch."

My house isn't that small. "I'm the person who called 911."

"Yes." The detective flipped the page. "What were you doing over here?"

"I'm the family doctor and counselor. I was working."

Joshua attempted to take a step around the detective, and the detective stepped in his way.

"Are you in a hurry?"

"May I please see Barbara? I am sure she needs me."

The detective flipped to a fresh page on his notepad. "Just a couple questions. Where were you just now?"

Joshua hesitated. He did not want Harold pulled into an impromptu interrogation.

"I was out back. Their son just saw his father shoot himself. You can understand how fragile both Barbara and her son are now."

"The lead detective will probably want to talk with him after he finishes with Barbara."

"I'm afraid I can't allow that. Harold's medical condition requires a calm environment. He is in no condition to talk today. Please, let me speak to Barbara, and then I'll talk to the detective and set up a time for him to be interviewed."

Detective Rodriguez slapped his notebook shut. "Please, wait here."

The detective left Joshua to wait. He felt like a stranger in the house he had called his second home just an hour earlier. He stood there attempting to contemplate the horror around him. *I can't believe Richard is dead.* They had just spoken that morning about Joshua's blog. Richard said he would consider setting up a video studio for him. *How could Richard just chat like nothing was wrong? He knew what he was planning. You're all about yourself, Joshua. You never really considered the lives of your patients—just their paychecks.* Joshua collapsed on the brown couch next to him and shook his head to stop the dark voice inside himself.

Detective Rodriguez returned and motioned Joshua toward the foyer. Barbara sat with kneeling policewomen on each side of the chair. They held her hands and spoke softly with her. A man with an air of being in charge stood against the wall. Joshua looked at the man's suit and thought all the detectives must have gotten their clothes from the same store, although his shoes seemed newer. Joshua guessed he must be the lead detective since he was the only one in the room. The detective spoke to Joshua as soon as he saw him.

"And what is your name, sir?"

"Dr. Joshua Zeev."

The detective pointed to the wall next to him. "Please stand over here with me, but don't say anything until I finish taking Mrs. Brown's statement."

Joshua walked over to the detective. His identification badge read *Louis Sanchez*. Detective Sanchez stood evenly with Joshua. Unlike Joshua's late fifties, the detective appeared to be at least ten years his junior. However, his demeanor gave the impression of someone much wiser for his age. Joshua continued to focus on reading the body language of the people in the room with Barbara and him. The normalcy of his activity felt like a warm blanket on an icy day. It distracted him from his own despair. He noticed both police officers with Barbara were genuinely empathetic. Detective Sanchez sounded all business, but the small twitch in his right eye told Joshua he was struggling with his emotions.

"Mrs. Brown, I believe you were telling me what you saw happen."

Barbara attempted to speak through her sobs. "I had just finished making myself a cup of tea. I was coming down the hall to Richard's office to check on him. We had talked the night before about possible layoffs at our company, and he was trying to figure out a way to save people's jobs. Part way down the hall, I heard the gun go off. I darted inside and found him dead in his chair. Harold was already there. He was very upset."

The head detective lowered his notepad with a concerned scowl. "Is there any chance Harold shot his father?"

"No, never. He was nowhere near the gun or his father when I stepped into the room."

Louis closed his notepad and shook his head. "Well, that's part of our problem, ma'am. We can't seem to locate the gun. Given where your husband was shot, we would expect to find the weapon on the floor."

Joshua turned to the detective and spoke up. "I'm afraid that's my fault. I found the gun and put it in the desk drawer after I took the bullets out."

He took the desk key and the bullets from his pocket and handed them to the officer.

The edge in Detective Sanchez's voice exposed a simmering anger. "Why would you touch anything? I realize you may be close to the family, but as a doctor, you must understand forensics."

Joshua looked the detective in the eye. "I do. However, their son is very upset, as you can tell by the office. I was concerned the young man might find the gun and take his own life, as well."

Sanchez brow wrinkled with concern. "Is he a danger? Do we need to take him into custody? Where is he?"

Joshua put up his hands and shook his head, "Oh, no, nothing like that! I can assure you as his psychiatrist, he'll be okay. He is—was—very close to his father. Seeing his dad take his life, who knows what decision someone might make in a moment of grief? I talked with him before everyone arrived. Yes, he is upset, any normal person would be, but he's not a danger to himself or others. I left him down by the pool. That area is very peaceful. He just needs privacy to mourn and process what he just saw."

"Thank you, Joshua," Barbara said in a strained voice.

The detective pointed to the officers by Barbara and then at the front door. Both officers left on cue. "I understand. You all have experienced enough today. I think we should probably give you folks time to catch your breaths. We might come back with more questions, depending on what we find."

"Of course, Detective," said Mrs. Brown. "Would you mind working with Joshua to make any arrangements? I don't feel up to dealing with these matters now."

"Of course, ma'am. I am sorry for your great loss. Oh, one other thing, and this is just routine. We do need to swab your hands, and Harold's, for GSR. This is perfectly normal, even in the case of a suicide."

"Do what you need to. Please, Joshua, accompany the police officer when they swab Harold. You can explain things better to him than they can. No offense, Detective."

"Of course, Mrs. Brown."

Joshua turned back to the detective. "May I please take Barbara into the kitchen now and get her something to drink? She needs some quiet."

"Please do. We're sorry to put everyone through this. Your family has been great for our community. However, with any shooting, we have to look at everything."

Joshua nodded, helped Barbara up, and escorted her to the kitchen. The police remained busy processing evidence at the other end of the estate. He made her a cup of tea and suggested they both go join Harold by the pool. Joshua would inform the detective where to find them to do their test. They were about to exit when Joshua noticed the note still in Barbara's hand.

"Barbara, the police will need that note."

Barbara hesitated and then handed the torn and bloodstained note to Joshua. "Okay, but please ask them if I may have it back."

Joshua took the note to Detective Sanchez. The detective informed him they would return the letter once the investigation concluded. When he returned to Barbara, they joined Harold by the pool. Barbara walked over to sit on the edge of the lounge chair beside Harold. He was looking up and seemed lost in the blue of the heavens. Harold stirred when Barbara sat down next to him. Mother and son held one another and cried some more.

Joshua walked away to be alone. Richard was a good friend—never someone Joshua viewed as a patient. Perhaps if he had, he could have seen this coming. He didn't know what the future held, but he knew the family needed him now more than ever.

He stood on the edge of the pool deck and watched the ambulance drive away, lights off. It carried away a good friend and father. The vehicle disappeared down the small lane that led off the hill. Joshua could feel whatever joy Richard's life had brought to the family disappear as the white and red ambulance faded from sight. His thoughts pulled him inside the shadows once more. *I failed him. My best friend, the man who would do anything for me, has killed himself, and I did nothing to prevent it. I just don't understand this. Shouldn't I understand this?*

He heard a noise to his side. A detective stood with three swabs in his gloved hand.

"I am Detective Jones. I'm sorry to interrupt. Just an FYI, the rooms with yellow tape can't be entered. I understand this is likely suicide, but until we make our final findings, it's treated as a possible murder. Also, I need a GSR sample from each of you. Just hold out your hands while I wipe them with this solution on the cotton swab."

Joshua held out his hands, and the detective swabbed them. The two of them walked over to Barbara and Harold. The detective followed the same procedure.

"That's fine. We have everything we need for now. I am sorry for your loss."

Joshua walked the detective up the path around the house and returned to Barbara and Harold once all the cars were gone. Mother and son sat arm in arm. Their eyes appeared distant as they silently stared toward the ocean below the hill.

"I'm going back inside the house to see what rooms the police sealed off," Joshua said.

He turned and walked back to the house. Everything felt lost. How could he help Barbara and Harold when he was not able to help himself? Dust in the air and roses from a nearby vase greeted Joshua when he entered. He found Richard's office door and the guest bedroom locked in place with yellow tape across them. The master bedroom located beside Richard's office was still accessible. Joshua thought it best to advise Barbara to take the guest master bedroom at the other end of the house next to Harold's bedroom. He would move into Maria's bedroom across from Harold and have Maria stay in his guest bedroom across the street at his house.

Joshua walked to the other end of the estate and peeked into Maria's bedroom. She sat on her bed with her head in her hands, gently sobbing.

He spoke softly to her. "Maria, I am sorry to bother you. This is such a grim time for us all."

Maria looked up. Her eyes and cheeks were red and puffy. "Yes."

"I'm sure you know both Harold and Barbara are very upset. I really need to be with them as much as possible."

Maria nodded. "I know. You are so good to think about them right now. I know you are hurting too."

"I don't think I'm good, but I'm worried about them both. Maria, I really hate to impose, but is it possible you could stay in the guest room at my home and let me stay here in your room, at least until the funeral is over?"

"Of course, but I've never been inside your house. I don't know where the bedrooms are."

"Don't worry. I'll show you. Are you able to pack while I help Barbara and Harold? I'll take you over in a little while."

"Of course."

Maria sniffed and wiped her eyes and nose with the weathered tissue she held.

Barbara and Harold came inside after a while and the three of them sat in the living room together. Although he could see the sadness in their eyes, Joshua guessed they had no tears left to cry that day.

"Barbara, why don't you move over to the guest suite nearer to Harold? I spoke with Maria. She has agreed to let me stay in her room, and she will stay in my home, at least until the funeral. I know I would feel better if we could all be near one another."

Barbara looked relieved. "Joshua, thank you. That sounds perfect."

"Okay, Doc. What can I do to help?"

Harold sounded like he needed a distraction.

"Can you help your mom move her things into the other bedroom after you clean up? I will take Maria across the street."

"Of course, I'll help Mom out. When will you be back over?"

"I shouldn't think it'll take more than an hour."

"Sounds good, Doc. Mom and I will go get things together in her room. We'll see you when you come back over."

All three stood up and left. Joshua went and poked his head into Maria's room. She was packed and typing on her small laptop at her desk.

"All ready, Maria?"

"Yes, are we going now?"

Joshua picked up her small bag. "Yes, we are. Please, come with me."

They walked across the street and up the short driveway to his front porch. His house was very modest by Malibu standards. For Joshua, it was a sanctuary. The bright white stucco looked beautiful in the sunlight. Its gold trim gave the ranch-style home a happy and cheerful feeling. Richard built him the Texas-sized front porch. He said it would not match the friendly porches of North Carolina, but it would provide room for their many friends to enjoy the ocean view.

He and Maria stepped inside the entryway. To their right was his living room. He rarely had an occasion to use this room. If an acquaintance appeared, they would simply sit on the front porch, but he still loved the room with its hardwood floors and grand brown oval rug. Several family antiques decorated the room: an old table, the sole survivor of his great uncle's house fire, sat against the far wall; a large spinning wheel and grandfather clock adorned two of the corners of the room. A beautiful red velvet couch with gold trim sat against the left wall and faced the front picture window. It was a showpiece that had belonged to his grandfather. Two handcrafted stuffed chairs graced the wall by the picture window. *Maybe I don't use this room because it's more of a museum.* He glanced over at Maria and caught her admiring the couch.

Joshua smiled. "If you would like to use this room, you may. I'm afraid it doesn't get much use."

Maria returned his smile and stared into Joshua's eyes. "Thank you, Joshua. I love this room."

Joshua showed her the rest of the house. Across from the living room was the hallway. He walked her into the front bedroom.

"This is your room. The bathroom just out your door and to the left is yours to use."

"This is perfect. Thank you so much."

"I should be thanking you. Allowing me to use your room is an immense help to all of us."

Maria bowed her head shyly. Joshua took her into the main part of the house. The dining room and family room existed in one large room together. The nine-foot ceilings made the house feel even larger. The kitchen sat just past the great room and dining area. Beyond the kitchen was the TV room where a fifty-inch television hung mounted on the wall. Joshua was a big Carolina Panthers fan. He and Richard used to bet and lose to one another whenever the Panthers would play a West Coast team. A pang of sadness hit Joshua at the thought. *I'm not sure I will ever be able to enjoy football again.* Everything seemed to point to his loss and failure.

"Are you okay, Joshua?" Maria asked.

Startled out of his thoughts, he looked and saw the concern on her face. "We're all sad today."

Maria lowered her head. "Yes."

Finished with the tour, Joshua left Maria to settle in. He walked back to the hall. Just past the guest room and bathroom was his home office. Joshua continued past that to his master bedroom at the end of the hall. He gathered enough clothes and toiletries for a week.

He could always walk back across if he forgot anything. Packed up, Joshua told Maria goodbye and returned to the home. He had just put his suitcase in Maria's bedroom when Harold poked his head in the door.

"Hey, Doc. Mom said she wanted to be left alone. To be honest, I do too. Are you okay on your own the rest of the day?"

"I am. You do whatever you feel you need to do. I'm here if you need me."

"Thanks, Doc."

With that, Harold walked back to his room and closed his door. Joshua heard him flip on his television. After he finished unpacking his suitcase, Joshua decided to go to his office. He chased his thoughts around his head. *I hope Barbara can survive this. She and Richard have always been a team. Why would Richard just leave her like this? Harry, what can I do to help you? I couldn't save my best friend. How am I going to get Harry through this?*

Locking the door, he collapsed on the couch and wept as he spoke into a pillow. "How could this have happened? What did I miss?"

He needed to write his thoughts down. Joshua started up his computer and began writing in his personal journal.

My best friend committed suicide today. Like so many others, he never hinted that he was considering taking his own life. His suicide note claimed there are answers on his laptop. How can anyone think there is an answer for taking their own life? If he had known his brains would splatter into the chair and wall behind him. If he had known his son would tear apart the room or that his wife would cry the day away, would he still have done this? I will never know. Why didn't he come to me? Why didn't he ask? He not only took his life, he did it in front of his son. Now I fear Harold has regressed. How can I call myself a psychiatrist if this is the result of my work? How am I going to find the truth when I don't even know who I am now?

Joshua dropped his hands from the keyboard and stared out the window. His mind wandered toward his business. *What will I put in my blog?*

The website was one of Richard's gifts to him when he agreed to become the family's long-term psychiatrist for Harold. Joshua closed his journal and started the programs he needed for his website. A web browser filled one monitor and a word processor filled the other. Despite the despair, Joshua smiled at the blog he had built over the last eighteen years. He had managed to gain a large following during that time. He quit counting when the numbers broke ten thousand readers. With the exposure came sponsors. He now made more money posting advice to users and interacting with his fellow psychiatrists than he did working for the Brown family.

Richard's gift not only provided Joshua with a self-sufficient income, but it had also helped millions of people over the years. Neither he nor Richard ever imagined it would grow into a global, self-supporting venture. Joshua's original intent was to keep his counseling skills up. It was meant as a reference for a new private practice when the day came for him to leave the Brown family. Joshua took a moment and opened his archive of articles. He glanced down the list and thought about how times back then seemed so simple. Colleagues from North Carolina would occasionally reference his work or send in seed questions for Joshua to answer.

Childhood development was his passion, but over the years that had grown into familial relationships. Joshua clicked on the menu titled "Surviving Your Family." The archived article was entitled "How to Survive an Angry Child." It had over twenty thousand likes and ten thousand shares. That article had changed everything. Word began to spread back east that an authored psychiatrist was offering free counsel to those who were willing to ask questions in a public forum. Soon psychologists and psychiatrists from all over were referencing his web pages on topics of rebellion, temperament, cognitive development, and others. Then the search engines began to pick up the links. Before long, Joshua had more people seeking out his advice and referencing his responses than he ever thought possible in a dozen practices.

Joshua smiled and thought of that part of his friend's legacy. Then he frowned, buried his head in his hands, and let the demons in his head overshadow his moment of light. *What counseling have I given to people over the years that's been wrong? How many others have died because I made a mistake? What do I write? How can I explain any of this or even how I'm doing? If I write what I'm really thinking, nobody will ever listen to me again. Maybe they shouldn't.* He knew he was in no condition to advise people right now.

I'm supposed to have the answers, but there are no answers to my nightmare. Why does God allow these things to happen? The question hung there in the silence, steeped in anger and grief.

Joshua put his arms on his desk and buried his head in them to muffle his cries. Everything he thought he knew, everyone he thought he'd helped, it was all an illusion. How had he missed Richard's depression? Richard blew his brains out in front of his son. A psychiatrist should not miss that kind of distress. Harold had not really improved since his childhood. He all but gutted Richard's office in a berserker rage. All his work over the last eighteen years seemed to have no meaning.

When Joshua awoke it was almost sunset. He stood and stretched. Joshua stared at the office that once had been his home away from home. *I know Richard is standing here looking and wondering why I'm feeling sorry for myself. His note said I'm supposed to do something.* A chill swept across his body, and Joshua shivered at his thought.

The pale-yellow walls and tiled floor had a grayish hue in the dying light of the day. The Southwestern décor felt as bland as the desert. The handmade rug given to him by Richard brought some warmth to his room. Joshua smiled at the memory. Richard paid a Native American woman of Chumash ancestry to make the red, black, and white rug. Joshua thanked Richard for giving him something other than pale yellow to decorate his office. They both laughed. Richard said Joshua's comment had been funny because it was true.

A tear rolled down Joshua's face. *Who can I laugh with now? Those moments between us died with you, my friend.* Another chill enveloped his body with the thought. He sat down on his old couch and closed his eyes. Joshua's soul ached to go back in time to the days before all of this began. He would give away everything he had gained for the chance to never have come to California to begin with.

He needed to talk to someone. Someone he could trust. Joshua thought of the one man he used to be as close to as Richard. Someone he had known before California and the Browns. A doctor who could not only console him but help take over his responsibilities for a while. He scanned his smartphone contacts and picked the name.

A North Carolina number began to ring.

"North Carolina Children's Home, Dr. Adam."

Joshua sat down in his chair. "Adam, this is Joshua."

"Joshua, I thought I wouldn't hear from you until our next conference."

"I'm afraid I have terrible news. Richard has taken his life."

"Oh no! I am so sorry to hear that. Is the family okay? Are you okay?"

"The family will need time. I'm afraid I'm not doing too well either. I feel like I've failed the family. I just need to know if my one successful patient is still okay. Adam, I need to know, have you heard from Bill?"

"No. The last I heard, he was living somewhere in North Carolina and is a successful investment banker."

"Do you know if his condition ever returned?"

"After you left, he never had a reoccurrence. Why? What's happened to Harold?"

Joshua felt relieved at Adam's news. He put his arm on his desk and rested his forehead on his palm.

"I'm not sure. He saw Richard shoot himself."

"Good Lord! What did he do?"

"He completely destroyed the office, except for his father's desk."

"Interesting. Did he hurt anyone or himself?"

Joshua stood and began to pace. "No, he moved Richard's body to a guest bedroom and then he calmed down. As calm as anyone can be when something like this happens. I honestly don't know what I'm going to do. What if Harold begins having random episodes again?"

"I can understand your concern, but I think he's okay. Even a completely normal person would have an extreme emotional response to seeing a loved one shoot themselves."

"Perhaps. Adam, I never saw any of this coming. I think I'm a total failure. I don't know, maybe not. I just don't feel qualified to give an opinion on anything right now. For all I know, Harry is doing as well as can be expected, or he is on the verge of a total relapse."

"Joshua, stop it. You are one of the best psychiatrists I know. You helped so many boys when you were here at the orphanage. Many of those young men are leading successful lives today because of you."

Joshua dropped onto the couch and punched a pillow. "Perhaps despite me."

"Please stop beating yourself up. You know that doesn't help."

"I don't know what I know. I really need time to work through all of this myself. I don't suppose you could do me a favor while I work through all of this?"

"Anything."

"Could you please take over my blog? I need time to grieve and help the family. I need time to help myself."

"Of course, my friend. Do you care what I write about?"

Joshua walked back to his desk and stood looking down at his computer screens. "Please don't mention anything about me. I think it might be good for our readers to learn about the orphanage and what you do."

Joshua dropped down into his chair.

"That's a wonderful idea. Don't worry about anything. Just send me your login information so I can post articles."

"I'll set you up as a guest author on the account as soon as I finish my post about my absence. Thank you again. This is a very difficult time."

"If you need me for anything, Joshua, please do not hesitate to call."

"Thank you. You're a great friend. Goodbye."

Joshua hung up the phone. He sat and stared out the window some more while he gathered his thoughts then turned back to his computer and began to type.

Dear friends, colleagues, and readers,

I have recently lost one of my closest friends. This man committed suicide. None of us (myself included) had any clue about his plans. I need to take a leave of absence while the family and I mourn and figure out our next steps. My good friend Dr. Adam from the North Carolina Children's Home will be writing in my absence.

Let me encourage you before I go: if you suffer from depression and ever think about taking your life, please call the National Suicide Prevention Lifeline: 1-800-273-8255. Believe me when I tell you that the loved ones you leave behind will suffer far worse than you currently are, no matter what you are going through today.

Dr. Joshua Zeev

Joshua bowed his head and prayed God would take away the horrible pain piercing their souls.

Chapter 2

Joshua opened his eyes slowly. Two Mexican rag dolls known as Marias sat on the white desk across from the twin bed he lay in. They both gave him empty, unblinking stares. *Where am I?* Everything began to flood into his mind. Richard was dead, and he was asleep in Maria's room in the family's house. Joshua slowly sat up and got his bearings. Looking over at the clock, he saw that the time was 6:45 a.m. The morning light was just beginning to invade the bedroom. He stood up and went over to his suitcase at the end of the bed to pick out some clothes. Quietly, he traveled down the hall to the bathroom. Joshua stood in front of the bathroom mirror.

Joshua looked into the mirror and spoke to himself, "Have I really aged this much in fifty-eight years?"

His thick locks that had once been jet black were now mostly gray. Deep wrinkles had formed between his dark brown eyes from hours of thinking. Although weighing 210 pounds was not huge for a man six feet tall, he recalled a time when he was twenty pounds lighter. He sighed and finished his morning routine. It seemed so meaningless. What could he do with his day? Still, he had to hide his personal pain for the sake of

Harold and Barbara. He may not be much of a psychiatrist, but he could still be a supportive friend. Joshua headed to the kitchen to make coffee.

He leaned against the indigo cabinets and waited for his coffee to finish brewing. The house was very quiet with Barbara and Harold asleep. Joshua opened the refrigerator and hunted for the cream. He missed his home even though it was only across the street. He knew where everything was in his refrigerator. Finally, he discovered the cream behind a milk carton.

I wonder what time Maria normally starts breakfast?

Joshua sipped his coffee for a moment and considered walking over to his house but then decided he did not want to startle Maria if she was just waking up—or worse, getting out of the shower.

He decided to head to his office. It was not home, but it was his personal space. None of his schooling or experience had prepared him for this. He stared at his computer screens, both turned off. He got up from his old mahogany desk and stared across the street at his home, missing the eggs and bacon he would be cooking right now.

He smiled and spoke to his empty office. "If it could only be that simple again."

His time dealing with Harold's temper felt mostly wasted. Eighteen years, and Harold still had fits of rage. How could he help the family? Sitting on his couch for a few moments, he bowed his head in prayer, but words failed him. He had failed; nothing could change that.

Joshua heard somebody in the kitchen getting a cup of coffee. Looking at his watch, he saw it was 8:00 a.m. How long had he been trying to pray? Joshua got up and went into the kitchen where he found Harold next to the coffee pot. He slid back a chair and joined him.

"Good morning. How are you doing?"

Harold held up one finger with his free hand while he poured his coffee. He walked over and grabbed the chair opposite of Joshua.

"I relive the same bad dream over and over. I keep seeing Dad pull his hand out from under the desk with the gun in it. Then he tells me to take care of Mom before sticking it in his mouth and pulling the trigger. I just wish I could go back in time and stop all of it."

"If you want to talk about it this morning in my office, I am here for you."

"I think I do, Doc."

"Care to join me now?"

"Sure, Doc."

Harold lumbered behind Joshua, his grief easily heard in his labored steps. Each one thundered with extraordinary effort. Inside Joshua's head his mind screamed, *What are you doing? You're a fraud! You know you can't help him. Your own friend killed himself. Stop wasting everyone's time.*

He clenched his fist and forced the thoughts away. They both sat down on the couch, facing the office door. Joshua turned and faced Harold.

"Tell me, what are you thinking about today?"

Harold turned and propped his left leg up on the couch. It had been a habit of his since he was a child meeting with Joshua. "It's like I told you in the kitchen, Doc. I watched my dad take his own life. He felt like there was a conspiracy against the company. He believed

Senator Jones was involved. Whoever the others are, Dad was convinced they wanted to suck the company dry of contracts until both the company and our family were bankrupt. Dad thought his death would interrupt their plans. That was the last thing he told me before taking his life, and I don't want to talk about that again."

Harold fidgeted on the couch in agitation as tears filled his eyes.

"Harry, help me understand. Your dad was my friend. We were confidants to one another. At least I thought we were. I'm trying to figure out how I didn't see this coming. I feel like I share responsibility in your dad's death."

"You didn't kill Dad, Doc. I think those men killed my dad."

"Harry, your father took his own life. Richard could have come to me. I would have helped him through this. I don't know why he didn't trust me."

Harold's large hand slammed down on the back of the couch. "No! They took it! He would never have killed himself if they hadn't tried to destroy everything he had ever worked for!"

"Why do you think they were targeting your father and his company?"

Harold's knee slid off the couch, and he bent forward. "They sacrificed our company just to make themselves richer. Those men claimed to be my dad's friends! They weren't his friends. They were just trying to get in close."

"Close to what?"

Joshua leaned toward Harold. He was growing concerned Harold might become paranoid while dealing with his father's death.

Harold sighed in frustration and turned his head to face Joshua. "Look, Doc, Dad told me a group of three people had gone into business together and were trying to take down our company."

"Why would they want to shut down the company?"

Harold sat back and put his leg up on the couch again. "He said he had information from a private detective. This information showed Senator Trey Jones was connected to some offshore businesses that are not listed on any reports to the US Senate or the IRS."

For a moment, Joshua forgot his own self-pity. "Did your dad say anything else? Is there something he wanted you to do?"

"He wanted me to try and stop them," Harold said in a cold, hard tone.

Joshua sat there for a moment, unsure how to take Harold's response and not sure he wanted to ask any more questions.

"Harry, tell me how you would stop them."

"If you're worried about me getting violent, I won't. Dad didn't want me to murder them. He wanted them stopped."

"How do you think you will do that?"

"I don't know yet. I have so many things to do. Mom isn't doing well, so I'm handling the funeral. Dad left written instructions with the board to have me approved as the new CEO. I got the email this morning. I want the position, but I don't know if I have time for that job and time to find these people."

Joshua took Harold's hand. "You have a lot on you, Harry. Of course, I don't understand what goes on with the company beyond the needs of a few employees. I will say you need time to mourn, and your mother needs your support. Believe me, if someone is behind this, I want them as much as you do, but you have to give yourself time."

Harold pulled his hand back. "You don't know half as much as you think you know."

Joshua clasped his own hands and leaned in toward Harold. "I am trying to understand. There is just something here that isn't making sense to me. Why are you so fixated on these men instead of your family? I—excuse me, we—will get them, but you need to take care of yourself and your family first."

"Doc, you just don't get it. Dad is expecting me to stop this. If we wait, we may still lose everything."

"Would you be willing to do a hypnotherapy session and see what I can learn?"

Harold shook his head. "Doc, I'm not a boy anymore. I don't think your fantasies can really resolve my father's suicide."

Joshua faced the door and leaned forward. His forehead wrinkled deep in thought. "Perhaps not. I would like to try though. It may help us both understand this better."

Harold shrugged. "Suit yourself. At least it will give me a break from my real nightmare."

Joshua got up, walked over to his desk, and picked up his pen. Returning to the couch, he held the pen up between Harold and himself.

"I want you to focus on the pen. There is only the pen. All your grief is leaving you now, leaving this room. You are safe here, just the two of us. Focus on the pen as I twist it back and forth. Feel yourself relaxing. There is nothing here but us and the pen. You are completely safe. We are leaving the room together. Focus on the pen as we walk together in the woods. Smell the trees, hear the birds. There is nothing but the forest floor."

Joshua could see Harold's eyes become glassier, and he slowly lowered the pen. Harold was under. Joshua's mind attempted to distract him again. *Why am I doing this? If his treatment worked so great, Richard's office would still be in one piece, but I must try.* Joshua didn't know which man living inside his head he hated more—the one who wanted to quit or the one who would not allow it.

"Tell me what you see, Harry."

Harold spoke with a voice like a child. "The woods. It's fall. It's beautiful. I like your white wolf skin and sword. I'm a bear, and I'm bigger than you."

"Yes, Harry, it's like you, a large, strong bear. Why are we here?"

Harold's brow wrinkled, and his glassy eyes narrowed into slits. His voice deepened into a threatening tone. "I'm here to destroy these men."

"What men, Harry?"

"Listen, I can hear them coming. Get your sword ready."

Harold stood up from the couch, and his eyes began to dart around.

Joshua asked, "Where are the men now?"

Harold pointed, starting left to right. "There, there, and there."

"Who are they, Harry?"

"You know, Doc. It's Senator Jones, Jerry Guilford, and John Richmond. We've been betrayed! Prepare yourself, Doc."

"What are they doing?"

"Beating their shields, but they look frightened. They are all smaller than me, and fatter. They think they look scary with their long hair and beards. They can't scare me."

Harold let out a howl and started panting. His right arm swung swiftly and deliberately at various angles.

"Harry? Harry, can you hear me?"

Harold's breaths slowed to long, deep breaths, and he was smiling.

"I got them, Doc. I took out all three. Do you see?"

Harold started pointing up and around the room.

"Over there is one head, and there's an arm, and another one right here. I destroyed them. They belong to the ravens now."

"How do you feel?"

Harold let himself plop down on the couch, and he slapped Joshua's knee with his large palm. "Good. My enemies are dead."

Joshua rubbed his knee but did not complain. "Why did they have to die, Harry?"

Harold's right arm hung partway up, resting on an unseen object. He leaned his body against his arm and turned to respond to Joshua.

"They had to be destroyed, or they would have destroyed us."

I need to get him past this. I must know what Richard told him right before he died. "What will you do now?"

A confused look passed across Harold's face. "I don't understand."

"You defeated your enemies. What will you do now?"

Harold smiled and spoke. "Guard against our enemies."

"What enemies are left, Harry?"

Harold shrugged. "I don't know."

He sat silent for a couple of minutes.

Joshua pressed his question again. "Harry, who are you going to guard against?"

"I don't guess anybody. I didn't think about that."

"Harry, who told you those men are evil?"

Harold's hand appeared to lay the invisible object against the couch, and he turned to face Joshua. "My dad. He's the chief. He told me right before they took him away. He hasn't been back since."

Joshua leaned toward Harold and lowered his voice. "Did he tell you why you had to defeat those men?"

"He said our spy Darla Johanson has the answers."

Darla. I must find out who she is. "Did he tell you if Darla told him anything else?"

Harold shook his head. "He said Jerry and John were planning to attack."

"I thought they were your friends. Did your dad say why he thought they would attack?"

Harold shrugged his shoulders. "I don't know."

"Okay, Harry. You will remember everything you told me. We are going to come back now." Joshua raised his pen. "The woods are falling away. The birds, the bodies, and the trees are fading. You see my pen before you. The office walls are returning. You can smell the interior of your home. You hear my voice in the room with you. When I snap my fingers, you will be back with me."

Joshua dropped his pen and snapped his fingers. Harold blinked his eyes in recognition. He sat there for a minute.

Joshua finally spoke. "How are you doing?"

Harold slumped his shoulders. "Better. I guess I didn't think about the future. I just wanted revenge."

Harold sounded a bit defeated.

"It's okay, Harry. If I'm honest, I want revenge, as well. I think you have some important decisions to make. I will be here if you need to talk some more."

Harold relaxed his leg on the couch again. "Doc, I think we should talk to Darla. Would you be willing to help me meet with Darla? I think we should work together on this. That way I won't do anything I'll regret."

Joshua shook his head. "I don't know, Harry. I don't think I've been much help to anyone. I lost your dad, and I don't know what to think about you."

"What do you mean, Doc?"

Joshua put his hand on Harold's broad shoulder. His brows creased in concern. "I haven't seen you that enraged since you were a child."

"Doc, I watched my dad shoot himself."

Harold turned, bowed his head, and sighed deeply.

"I'm sorry, Harry. I need to stop feeling sorry for myself. All I can seem to think about is how I failed your father and whether I failed you. You lost your father and Barbara her husband. I should be focused on your needs first right now."

Harold raised his head and gave Joshua a half smile before responding. "Thanks, Doc. It sounds like we all have a lot to think about."

Joshua leaned back with a faint smile. "Harry, you're beginning to sound wise beyond your years."

Harold stood up. "It's from hanging out with an old man all my life."

They both chuckled.

Harold left Joshua's office. Joshua sat there fighting the conflict of his own self-pity and the revelations from Harold's session. *What if there is some sort of collusion? There can't be. It's so improbable.* He took a deep breath and looked out his window at the Malibu hills as he considered the second possibility. *What if everything Harry just said is simply ideas hiding in his head? What if it's all false? The subconscious mind can often play tricks on somebody's memories, especially when it's grieving. I just hope Harry's brain is not breaking under the stress.*

There was no way to tell yet if Harold's thoughts were just fantasy or real memories. However, if they waited too long, most of Harold's memories of Richard's suicide could disappear. This reminded Joshua of the promise he made the detective. He needed to make that appointment for Harold's interview. Whatever time they needed Harold, Joshua would make sure he was in the room so there would be less pressure. He picked up the phone and dialed the number.

"Malibu Police, Lead Detective Sanchez speaking."

"Detective, this is Dr. Joshua Zeev. We spoke yesterday."

"Of course. How is everyone holding up, Doctor?"

"About as well as can be expected. If you still need to interview Harold, I believe he can handle that now if I am in the room. I just ask it not take too long. Barbara is not doing well, so Harold is having to handle all the funeral arrangements."

"Doctor, I don't think I will need to speak with him. All the GSR tests were negative. Barbara's statement clearly puts Harold on the opposite end of the room. There is no way he could have shot the gun from there based on the angle of the bullet. We did some cursory checks into the company finances. At best, Parabolic Defense Systems has a year left before they run out of money. According to the report, Senator Trey Jones led the fight to cancel contracts and move them over to two other companies. I don't know if he had a falling out with Richard, but whatever it was, it really hurt the company. I guess it was more than Richard could take. I'm sorry he didn't come to you before pulling the trigger."

"Nobody is sorrier than me. Thank you, Detective. I'm sure Harold will be happy to miss the interview given what he is dealing with."

"Good luck, Doctor. I pray things get better for you and the Browns. They're a good family. I hate that this happened to them."

"Thank you. One last thing, Detective. When can we get into the rooms to have them cleaned?"

"Let me check with the lab. I have your email on your statement. I'll just email you and tell you what they say, if that's okay."

"Perfect. Thank you, Detective. Goodbye."

There it is. You see. I knew this would happen. Everyone knows you're a fraud, a failure. You just got lucky with Bill, but you can't handle the real cases.

He had to get out of the room, away from his own thoughts. Joshua walked into the kitchen to get another cup of coffee. Maria was there working on a meal.

"Good morning, Maria. I didn't hear you come in."

Maria turned around. Her smile washed away the demons in Joshua's head. "Good morning, Joshua. I tried not to disturb anyone."

Joshua leaned up against the kitchen island. "Did you sleep okay?"

Maria rested against the counter and gave Joshua her full attention. "I slept wonderfully. Your house is very nice. I do have a question. Why do you have black panther banners on the wall by the television?"

Joshua laughed. "It's my football team. Um, American football team. They play in North Carolina where I used to live."

Maria cocked her head slightly to the left and gave Joshua a playful grin before she spoke. "You don't like California football?"

"I do, but you always cheer for the team that's based where you're from. Are you making brunch?"

Maria turned back to her cooking and talked over her shoulder. "Yes, for Miss Barbara. She won't leave her room. I knock on the door and she screams I should go away, but she has to eat."

"I will try and take it into her. Let me grab some coffee, and I'll be back in a minute."

"Okay, it should be ready in five minutes."

Joshua poured his coffee, grabbed some cream, and headed to Harold's room. He could hear typing coming from inside. Joshua knocked on the bedroom door. The typing from inside the room stopped, and he could hear Harold's heavy steps coming to the door.

"Hey, Doc. What can I do for you?"

"I just wanted to let you know that I talked with the detective, and you shouldn't have to be interviewed."

"Thanks, Doc. That's one less headache in the murky world of headaches."

"One other thing, Harry. He did say we should be able to get into the rooms soon to clean them up."

Harold shook his head emphatically. "No, Doc. We aren't. At least, not now. It's too soon. I can't bear to open them."

Joshua reached up and gave Harold's massive bicep a squeeze. "Harry, the smell is going to get pretty bad. You may have to rip up all the floorboards and tear out the walls, at least in the office."

Harold kept shaking his head. "I don't care, Doc. I may do that anyway. I just don't want to look in there now. It's too soon."

"I didn't mean today, Harry, but don't put it off too long. Also, I am worried about your mom. Maria said she yelled at her to stay out and won't eat anything. I'm concerned she may give up on living. Are you okay with me talking with her?"

Harold's posture relaxed. "You can always talk to her, Doc."

"I know, but I am going to have to go into her bedroom even if she says no. I need to force her to interact with people before she closes up inside."

"Do anything you need to, Doc. Mom is the only family I have left."

Joshua left Harold's room. The voices in his head started back up. *You know you are just being cruel, forcing your way into her bedroom. Why don't you leave her alone? So, what if she stays like she is? Maybe that's what's best.*

Joshua knew that was not the right answer. He scowled to himself until he entered the kitchen and saw Maria. She had prepared a beautiful tray of local fruit, a poached egg, and two strips of bacon—one of Barbara's favorite meals. Maria's love for the family was his one bright spot in a dark morning.

"It's beautiful, Maria. If she doesn't eat it, I will."

Maria giggled. Joshua smiled, took the tray, and headed back down the hall. He knocked on Barbara's door.

"Leave me alone!"

Joshua faced the door and raised his voice. "Barbara, it's Joshua. I brought you some breakfast. It's your favorite."

"I'm not hungry!"

Joshua was not going to let her win. "Maria made it especially for you. She is worried about you. We all are."

"I'm fine. Now go away!"

Joshua thought for a moment. *So, you are doing it the hard way? Yes.*

He grabbed the doorknob. "I'm coming in. Cover up quickly if you need to."

Joshua opened the door. He was glad he turned his back toward Barbara. A pillow softly landed against him and hit the ground.

"You are a bit too predictable, Mrs. Brown. Please don't do that again. I don't want to drop this beautiful tray Maria worked so hard on."

Joshua looked over his shoulder. He worked hard to hide his shock. Barbara obviously had not slept at all. She looked like she had been in a boxing match. The darkness under her eyes reflected her shattered heart. Her hair sat atop her head in a tangled, matted disaster. One side of her face was bright red with a handprint. He wondered how long she had been resting her head on her hand.

Standing there, Joshua attempted to improve the situation. "Barbara, would you at least let me bring the tray over to the nightstand?"

"Okay, if it makes you feel better."

If only taking a tray of food to a friend could make me feel better ...

Joshua brought the tray over and set it down. He walked to the desk against the wall and took its chair. With a look full of compassion, he sat next to Barbara's king-size bed.

"I know you're hurting. You don't have to hide in here. Harold and I love you and want to be here for you."

Barbara adjusted her pillows and leaned back against the headboard. "I know. Joshua, you have always been good to my family. You and Richard just seemed to have so much in common. You loved to swim. I still remember the time you both took Harold to the beach when he was ten, and he found himself in a rip current. Richard saved Harold and you saved Richard. You three came back laughing about it. I was so afraid I would lose you all one day to your antics, and now I have lost Richard!"

She began to weep. Joshua moved next to her on the bed and held her while she cried. Inside Joshua was wailing too. *Why, God? Why couldn't I stop any of this from happening?* After a few minutes, she calmed down again. Joshua moved back to his seat.

"Barbara, you still have Harold and me. Harold needs you more than ever. He sees you as the only family he has left. I know it's hard, but you need to try and get moving. At least eat something. That will make us both feel better."

Joshua handed Barbara a tissue off the nightstand.

She cleaned the fresh tears from her cheeks. "Okay. I suppose you both will haunt me until I do. Hand me the tray."

Barbara began to nibble, and then her hunger took control, and she devoured everything on the plate. Joshua sat quietly while she did. When the plate was empty, she looked up.

"Are you satisfied, Doctor?"

Joshua smiled. "I am."

Placing the cloth napkin on the tray, she handed it to Joshua. "Good. Leave me in peace now. Tell Maria she may bring me tea and dinner every day but not to bother me otherwise."

Joshua placed the tray back on the nightstand. "Barbara, we need to discuss the funeral."

Barbara straightened the sheets covering her body. "There is nothing to discuss."

Joshua held her hand. "Please, Barbara. Don't you want to allow your friends time to honor Richard?"

She jerked her hand back. "I can't possibly think about that. I won't think about that!"

"Okay, Barbara. Harold is managing things. I will let him know he needs to continue handling things. I can help out where he needs me."

Barbara pointed toward the tray and then the door as she spoke. "Thank you, Joshua. Close the door on your way out."

Joshua closed the door behind him. He walked the five steps to Harold's door and knocked.

"Come in, Doc."

Harold was at his desk working on his computer. "Is my knock that distinctive?"

Harold turned around to face Joshua. "Yeah. How's Mom?"

Joshua leaned up against the wall. He felt as if he had just wrestled with a gorilla. "Grieving. She is leaving the funeral in your hands. I can help if you want me to."

"Thanks, Doc. I already saw this coming. Mom is not herself. I called my old buddy Tom to help."

"How did he take the news?"

"He is pretty torn up about my dad. Tom said he will do anything he can for the family. We're going to the funeral home together. I won't be gone long. I just need to pick out a proper casket. Mom and Dad already have plots. I'm not sure what to do about a minister. We have our family church, but I've never been close to anyone there really. To me, you've been the spiritual conscience of our family. Would you consider giving a eulogy?"

"I don't feel capable, but if you are sure, I'm honored to do so."

"Great. One other thing. I spoke with Darla Johanson about Dad. She wants to meet. The funeral is Saturday. That gives us four days before the funeral. I am thinking about having her come in Thursday to meet with us. I honestly think I can handle saying goodbye to Dad more easily if I understand what was going on."

Harold's idea stuck in Joshua's head. "I agree."

"You said you would be willing to help me out. Are you up to meeting with us?"

Joshua pushed himself off the wall. "I wouldn't miss meeting with you and Darla for anything. I have my own questions for Ms. Johanson."

"That works for me. I will email her and set up a 10:00 a.m. meeting. Talk with you later, Doc."

Joshua got up and left the room and dropped of the tray in the kitchen. He ran into Maria in the living room and relayed Barbara's message. She was ecstatic. Seeing Maria so happy lifted the heaviness on his shoulders for a moment. Joshua walked out through the French doors and onto the sundeck. He sat at a table. What would he say in memory of his closest friend who shot himself? He could not shake the feeling he was a hypocrite for agreeing to speak.

Joshua looked out toward the blue Pacific waters and spoke to the air. "Hi, everyone. I'm Joshua. I was Rich's closest friend and psychiatrist. I had no clue he was depressed."

He hoped Thursday would bring him some answers.

Chapter 3

Joshua sat with Harold at the breakfast table. Darla was due to arrive in thirty minutes. In front of them, Richard's old laptop sat with its lid closed. Harold had retrieved it from the police station now that they had officially declared his father's death a suicide. The rest of Richard's belongings that had been taken by the police sat in boxes in the garage.

"I have to admit, Harry, I'm out of my element. I've counseled people at the company, but I never dove into your dad's business dealings."

Harold leaned back in his chair and faced Joshua. "Don't worry, Doc. It really isn't too complicated. Dad started building rocket parts for the space program about ten years ago."

Joshua interrupted. "You can skip this, Harry. I know the company's history. I'm trying to understand what he was working on now."

Harold nodded. "Okay. Well, Parabolic Defense Systems had a string of defense contracts awarded for missile-based weapons, mostly tactical nuclear devices. The design is to lower nuclear fallout and minimize environmental and civilian casualties. Personally, I'm not sure how the government defines that, but less radiation is always better."

Joshua's mind kicked in. *A string of contracts? Richard told me he had only a couple of large projects just a month ago. Was he trying to hide something from me?*

"Harry, please don't take this question the wrong way. Is there any chance your dad was doing something he shouldn't have been? You said the company was awarded a string of defense contracts. Is that unusual?"

Harold thought for a moment. "I don't think so, Doc. I think we just offered the best deal. Our previous projects always ended on time or early, and we had no budget overruns. Dad told me the company stayed competitive by taking care of our employees. Parabolic doesn't give the highest salaries in the area, but the wages are fair. He made sure everyone had health care and promised them he would lose his job before they lost theirs. That's really all I know. Top secret bids are blind. Nobody is supposed to know why another company was picked, but there are always rumors."

Joshua sat back, folded his arms, and scowled at the computer. "Did Richard ever mention whether rumors were spread about the company?"

Harold shook his head. "Not that Dad heard."

"Harry, should we take a look now or wait for Darla?"

Harold turned his attention to the laptop. "Let's open it and see what's on here, at least."

He opened the lid and turned it on. A password prompt came up, and Harold typed in the password.

Joshua raised his eyebrows. "Your father gave you his password?"

"Yeah. I should have seen the clues, Doc. He gave me the password the day before he died. He said it was in case of an emergency. I never thought twice about it."

The laptop booted up. To their surprise, a folder sat on the desktop labeled "Harold and Joshua." Inside the folder, they found several saved emails. Both men read through them.

Richard,

You know my hands are tied. Yes, you were awarded the contract, but we reserve the right to cancel at the behest of the American taxpayer. Both Guilford and Richmond have offered less expensive nonnuclear options. I realize we never approached Parabolic about that option, but that's politics. The committee already voted and approved killing this project in favor of the other. I know we will do plenty of business in the future.

Sincerely,
Senator Jones

Joshua drew in a long, deep breath. He understood Harold's accusations now. Something had happened, but this email was no proof. It only led to speculation. Other emails included heated exchanges between Richard and the other two men. While all the emails appeared carefully worded, one did catch Joshua's attention.

Richard,

Yes, it is true. Richmond and I met with Senator Jones. That isn't unusual. You take him to dinner anytime he is in the state. Don't blame us if we beat you at your own game. We never asked for your projects to be canceled. Perhaps the senator sees the value of conventional advanced weaponry over a nuclear holocaust. I would suggest going back to the drawing board and focusing on coming up with something worth funding.

Sincerely,

Jerry Guilford
CEO, Guilford Defense Systems

Harold and Joshua looked at each other and then reread the emails. Harold sat there staring at the screen.

"This is what Dad was trying to warn me about. He must have thought the other two companies were in partnership with the senator."

"It does look suspicious, but I don't see anything here that indicates a conspiracy. Jerry seems a bit snarky for some reason. After all, his family has been over here many times for parties. I would have expected something a little more compassionate. There's almost a hatred in his tone."

"That last email must be after Dad talked with Darla. She should be here soon. Where do you want to meet?"

"We could use my office, but I think the conversation could become intense. Why don't we sit on the sundeck where the atmosphere is more relaxed?"

"That works for me, Doc. Will you please find Maria and tell her to bring Darla to the deck when she arrives? I'll meet you outside."

Joshua got up and went looking for Maria. Based on her usual schedule, she would be in the entertainment room dusting. He stopped, leaned against the doorway, and watched Maria wipe down the beautiful oak bar. Glass shelves supported the different liquor glasses under accent lighting. Bottles lined the counter, and wine glasses hung from the rack over the bar. It gave the air of an old western bar sitting amidst a multimillion-dollar estate. Maria did not see Joshua standing there. Her diligent concentration left a mirrorlike shine on the finish over the wood.

Joshua cleared his throat. "Excuse me."

Maria startled and turned. "Oh, I didn't see you standing there, Joshua."

He pushed himself off the doorframe and walked over to the bar. "I was appreciating your diligence. I need a favor, if you have the time."

Maria placed her rag on the bar and slid onto a stool. "I would be happy to. What do you need me to do?"

"A woman named Darla Johanson is coming to meet with Harold and me. When she arrives, would you please bring her out to the back deck? We're expecting her."

"Of course."

"How is Barbara?"

"She seems to be doing a little better. She was at her desk this morning when I brought in her food."

"I'm happy to hear that." Joshua reached over and touched her shoulder. "Thank you, Maria."

Maria smiled bashfully.

Joshua walked out. Harold was not outside yet. He sat down at the table, stretched out his legs, and let out a long sigh. It was a relief to have a minute to catch his breath. The ocean air smelled good. The cool breeze gently rolled up the slope and lifted the weight off Joshua's shoulders. Maria always seemed to make him feel better, for some reason.

Why have I not noticed how she brightens my day? Maybe it's my grief, but I could sit all day and listen to her talk. Come on now, Joshua, you know you love your psychiatry first. Too bad you failed. No, not this time. Maria has nothing to do with your shame.

Maria was more than ten years his junior. Although a humble woman and a faithful housekeeper, she carried with her the beauty and fire of all Hispanic women. Joshua began to wonder if it was time to focus on more important matters than his career. He was finally starting to fully relax when the French doors opened. Harold's body filled the doorway.

"Hey, Doc. Maria knows where to bring Darla?"

"Yes. Have you found anything else on the computer?"

"I haven't had time to look. I was talking with Tom about the funeral. I'm going to have him speak, and then I'll follow. We will have you deliver the eulogy last. Is your message ready?"

Joshua looked away from Harold, afraid he would see the uncertainty in his eyes. "It will be, God willing."

"Good, Doc. Let me get this laptop booted up again. Darla should be here any minute."

Harold disappeared back inside the house for a moment and reemerged with the computer. Both men scanned through the documents folder together.

"Well, Doc, I don't see anything else here about the contracts. There are lots of important files I need for Parabolic, but nothing else is jumping out."

Joshua leaned back in his chair. "Hopefully Darla can tell us more."

Maria opened the doors to the house. "Gentlemen, this is Darla Johanson. Ms. Johanson, that is Harold Brown and Dr. Joshua Zeev."

Joshua and Harold stood. Joshua immediately regretted his age. Darla was a raven-haired beauty in her early thirties and around five feet ten. She wore a tight business dress that accentuated curves and would catch the eye of the most pious of men. He caught himself staring, hoping he had not gotten caught. It did not matter; Darla's deep, dark eyes locked with Harold's. To Joshua's surprise, Harold had the look of a man sizing up his prey. Joshua looked over at Maria. She gave him a smirk and walked back inside.

Harold did not wait for anyone to sit down but spoke up immediately. "Ms. Johanson, what exactly did you tell my father?"

Darla pulled back her handshake. "You get right to the point. Good to meet you too."

Harold's glare did not waver. He crossed his arms, determined to get a response.

"I want to know what you both spoke about. Other than myself, you were the last person he spoke to about the trouble the company was in. What could you have told him to make him feel so helpless?"

"Perhaps we should sit down first," Joshua said.

Darla broke her icy stare from Harold. "Dr. Zeev, a pleasure."

She shook Joshua's hand. Her hand felt soft and cool, but Joshua could feel the strength in her grip. He had no doubt she could break every bone in his hand if she cared to. Harold took his seat, and the staring contest continued.

Darla placed her hands on the table. They lay in place without so much as a quiver. Her bravery impressed Joshua, although Harold seemed not to notice.

"Mr. Brown. May I call you Harold?"

"Not yet."

"Mr. Brown, your father and I had been investigating Senator Jones and CEOs Richmond and Guilford."

Harold leaned in toward Darla. She did not respond but held her position and pose despite his imposing posture.

"Yes, my dad told me they were after the company the day he died. I also have an email exchange between him, the senator, and Guilford. But that doesn't tell me why he would want to take his own life."

Darla touched the top of Harold's hand momentarily. "I am sorry for your loss. We had only worked together for a few weeks, but I feel his loss, as well."

Harold gave a slight nod. "Thank you. Please continue with what happened."

"After that email, he called me. I told him we had to move fast if we wanted to stop them. That night I was working on a lead for an offshore company in the Caymans. I believe it is one of three shell companies these men are using to funnel money from both Guilford Defense Systems and JR Aerospace. The CEOs of both companies have shares in these shell corporations. These corporations combined hold almost half of the stock in both defense companies."

"Where does the senator come in?"

"I don't how yet. I know only what you know. The senator met with these men and then suddenly started pushing the committee to reevaluate their contracts. Richard thought it could be a partnership. I tend to think it's blackmail. The senator has been in his position for twelve years. He heads the Armed Services Committee. Senator Jones has no need to siphon money from a defense contractor."

Harold sat back in his chair. "Okay, I can buy that. You still aren't telling me about my dad."

Darla put her hands in her lap and relaxed her posture. "As I was saying, I was on the trail of these companies, and then your dad got a phone call. John Richmond called and offered to buy out Parabolic. It wasn't a good offer, but it was fair. It came with a poison pill though. Richmond intended to lay off half of the employees and merge the two companies together. Your dad was livid and refused. Richmond told him his board would gladly take the offer in a week and likely fire him for turning it down."

"How do you know this?"

"Your dad requested I bug his phone. I couldn't get him the information he needed in a week, even with my leads. Technically speaking, private men owning shell companies and cashing in on two US companies is not illegal unless there was money laundering somewhere along the way. If the senator is involved, then everything changes. The senator would be lucky not to go to jail. If it is blackmail, of course, Guilford and Richmond will go to prison. I couldn't prove the conspiracy then, and I still can't."

Harold sat up. She obviously had his attention and Joshua's.

"Have you continued working on it?" Harold asked.

Darla shook her head. "Honestly, no. With your dad's suicide, I wasn't sure what you and your mother would do. I didn't want to possibly keep this wound open longer than it needs to be."

Harold relaxed his stare and stretched his arms over his head. He turned and looked at Joshua. "Doc, what do you think?"

Joshua shook his head. "I think I understand your dad's decision a little better. I don't agree with it, but I understand it. Still, he had options. There's a lot more we don't know, from the sounds of it. Darla, how long will it take to gather evidence on Senator Jones?"

Darla faced Joshua. "Well, Doctor, I don't want to go into too much. I have heard he is going on vacation to a secluded island near Key West. I think if the senator is involved, I may find some answers there."

Joshua's forehead wrinkled into well-worn creases as he thought. He looked back and forth at Darla and Harold. "Richard had money and lawyers. He could have bought the time he needed to bring this into the open. Something else had to have caused his death."

Darla took both men's hands. "I wish I could give you both an answer. My gut is telling me there is a lot more here than I have found."

She released their hands and sat back.

Everyone sat lost in thought for a moment. Harold sat up like someone had tapped him on the shoulder. Darla jumped.

"This may sound like a random question, but I'm curious," Harold said. "I've never met someone I couldn't intimidate. My own mother won't look me in the eye when I glare at her. Not only did you not flinch, you took me on eye to eye. What is your background?"

Darla straightened her posture and looked at Harold as though he was the only man on the sundeck. "US Marine Corps. Intelligence. After that, I worked for the CIA as an analyst and a couple other things."

Harold could not hide his surprise. "You quit the CIA?"

"Let's just say I was in North Africa and didn't like what I saw there at the time. So I walked."

Harold smiled. "Would you consider working for me like you did my dad? I will cover your trip to the Keys. Just bring me back something more than tan lines."

Darla looked annoyed at the quip. "I can assure you, Harold, I am quite proficient at my job. If you doubt me, please find someone else."

Harold raised his hands in a mocking defense gesture. "Easy, Darla. I trust you, otherwise I wouldn't have made the offer. Do you need any additional security?"

Darla smiled. "No. I'm a big girl and can take care of myself."

Harold lowered his arms and leaned close to her. "I bet you can."

Darla gave a sideways grin. "You would be surprised."

"Excuse me." Joshua mockingly raised his hand. "If you don't mind me interrupting your flirting, we still have a problem: timing. Your dad's death may buy us a few days, but Richmond will eventually try and buy the company."

Harold sat for a moment, looking at Joshua while he thought. "I think I can buy us a month with the board. Is that enough time, Darla?"

Darla smirked and nodded her head. "I can probably beat that timeline if the rumors I have heard are true."

Harold leaned a little closer to her. "Care to share those rumors?"

She shook her head. "No. They're pretty disturbing. Part of me hopes it's all a hoax and that the senator's involvement is purely political timing instead of something more nefarious."

Joshua sat back in his chair. "What sort of rumors?"

Darla turned to Joshua. "Doctor, I'm sure you hear all sorts of crazy stories."

Harold chuckled. "His primary job is taking care of our family, so I know he does."

Joshua smiled. "Ms. Johanson, I want to be involved here. Something these men did caused my best friend to end his life. Whatever impacts this family impacts me."

"I've told you everything I can at the moment."

Joshua shook his head and sat up on the edge of his chair. "You misunderstand me. I want to be involved.

I don't know what these rumors are, but I want to go with you and find out. I may look like a middle-aged bookworm, but I'm well traveled. A second set of eyes never hurts."

Darla shook her head. "No. That would put me in far too much danger. I will call as soon as I return to California. If you don't hear from me in thirty days, assume the worst and send someone to look for me."

Harold gave a boyish smile. "I will come myself."

Joshua was a bit surprised. Harold had never been a lady's man. Darla was certainly beautiful, but he hoped it was not Harold's grief talking. He refocused on their discussion.

Joshua looked at Darla and Harold, and his voice began to get louder as he spoke. "Darla, I'm not giving you a choice. Harry, if you want me to help, then you have to let me go with Darla."

Joshua's sudden insistence surprised them both.

Harold reached across with his long arm, and Joshua's hand disappeared inside of his. "Doc, I'm not sure you are up for this. Besides, I need you here for the funeral."

Joshua's shoulders slumped down. He could not refuse to help Harold with the funeral. "Very well. Ms. Johanson, please contact me if there is any way I can help."

"Please, call me Darla. Gentlemen, if you are done with me, I need to get moving. I have to pack and get a plane to Key West by tomorrow."

Both men rose, and Harold walked her to the front door. Joshua sat back down and stared out at the ocean vista. He was certainly out of his element. Trying to heal people was his specialty. *You're a psychiatrist, not a detective. Your healing talents are not all that strong either.* Joshua sighed and prayed for the day the critical inner voice would disappear.

Richard's suicide may have been due to desperation instead of depression. That still doesn't explain why Richard wouldn't come to me. We were best friends—like brothers. If Richard couldn't come to me for help, who can? There must be more going on. I need to find a way to join Darla. He needed answers. *Am I out of my element? After all, my whole life has been the study of human nature. Maybe I'm not a good counselor, but I know the human animal. Certainly, I can be an asset to Darla.*

Harold walked back outside and sat down. Joshua leaned close to Harold and looked him firmly in the eye.

"Harry, I really need to go with Darla. I must understand what your dad was thinking. I know the answers are on that island with those men."

Harold gave Joshua's shoulder a squeeze. "I know, Doc, but you help me to keep my head on straight."

Joshua leaned back and shook his head. "I do what I can, but I don't feel like it's enough."

"What are you talking about, Doc? Maybe you can't see it, but inside I know I'm far better off for growing up with you."

"Thanks, Harry. Promise me one thing. If Darla calls for me, you're okay with me flying back east."

Joshua could see the concern in Harold's eyes. "Doc, for years you have tried to bring me peace. If this trip means that much, then yeah. If Darla calls, go do what you think you need to do. I can manage alone for a few days."

"Thank you." The tension from the morning released, and Joshua stretched out his legs. He thought it was an appropriate time to finally refocus on other matters. "If I may change subjects, what are the plans for the funeral? Besides us speaking."

Harold stretched out his legs toward Joshua and clasped his hands behind his head. "The services will be held at Malibu Presbyterian. All the arrangements have been made. We just have to talk Mom into going."

Joshua sat up, his curiosity getting the better of him. "Do you have something in mind?"

Harold sat up, and a slight smile escaped his lips. "Well, Doc, I didn't want to tell you about a project Maria has been working on. What's that old saying, 'It's better to ask forgiveness than permission'? She's been sewing a special dress for Mom. I promise none of her sewing equipment hurt your football mementos."

Joshua laughed. "How many people do you have in my home?"

"Just Maria. She has been leaving after her morning cleaning to work on the dress. She shows up with Mom's food in the evening. Nobody has known our little secret, until now. I trust you can keep it."

Joshua winked. "I believe it falls under doctor-patient privilege."

"Good. Tomorrow morning, I would like you to join Maria and me in the kitchen at nine o'clock. We are all going to approach Mom together. Trust me, she can't say no to Maria's dress. It's stunning."

Joshua's had to smile at Harold's secret. It appeared there were many secrets floating around him, and not all were evil.

He stood as he responded, "I like your plan. Maybe you should have my job."

"No thanks, Doc. Then I would have to put up with people like me."

Joshua laughed and headed into his office. He hoped the message for his dead friend would reveal itself.

Chapter 4

THE NEXT MORNING, Joshua left his office at 8:30 a.m. and went into the kitchen to get one last cup of coffee before going in to talk to Barbara with Harold and Maria. He was surprised to find both already sitting at the kitchen table, talking.

Maria spoke first. "Good morning, Joshua."

Joshua smiled. "Good morning, Maria. It's good to see you this morning."

He and Maria stared at each other.

"Do I need to go to the other room?" Harold joked.

"I don't think that will be necessary," Joshua responded with a slight scowl.

"Joshua, would you like to see the dress that I made for Miss Barbara?"

"I would love to."

Intricate black lace covered the entire dress. Joshua had no idea how many hours Maria had spent, but he guessed she did not sleep as well as she claimed. Maria held up the veil, which would cover Barbara's face and drape down to her shoulders.

"That is one of the most beautiful dresses I have ever seen!"

Joshua knew he was a little too enthusiastic.

"Maria, you always do terrific work," Harold said. "I know Mom cannot say no to that dress. I guess we can just sit here and make small talk and look at each other awkwardly, or we could risk knocking on the door a little early. I heard her moving around in there an hour ago."

Maria responded, "I think we should go encourage her now."

Harold and Joshua agreed. They walked down the hall, and Harold knocked on her door.

"Harry, you may come in."

Harold opened the door and peeked inside. "Hi, Momma. May we please come in?"

"Yes."

His mother sat at a small desk. She had been writing, and from the looks of the stack of papers, she had been writing a lot. Barbara turned in her chair to face the group. Although her black circles remained, they had faded. Her freshly washed black hair rolled down over her shoulders once more. She had on one of her typical blouses and slacks. Joshua wondered why she remained in her room. She appeared ready to face the world again.

"I guess you can all see I've been a busy woman."

"Yes, ma'am," Harold said.

Barbara laid down her pen and turned to the small group. "I have been writing down everything Richard told me in his last week. I'm trying to figure out why the love of my life would leave me alone like this. I think it has something to do with Jerry and John. Richard said they were trying to steal our contracts. I happened to remember hearing Richard argue with

John Richmond on the phone the night before he died."

Joshua wondered how Barbara knew about the three men.

Harold's voice was soft as he spoke. "It's okay, Momma. Joshua and I are looking into that. We are all here about the funeral."

"Oh! I've decided to stay home."

"Barbara, we know this is hard," Joshua said empathetically "There are a lot of friends who want to see you and support you. If you aren't there, everyone will be asking Harry where you are. What will he tell them?"

"Oh, I don't care, Joshua. Harold is a smart son. He will think of something."

Harold pointed toward Maria. "Momma, Maria made you something just for the funeral. She worked on it day and night."

Maria stepped up and held up her dress. Barbara started to cry.

"Maria, that is so beautiful."

Maria lowered the dress and looked at Barbara with tears in her eyes. "It is beautiful just like you, Miss Barbara. You need to say goodbye to Mr. Richard, and I know he would love you in this."

The two women cried together. Joshua and Harold sniffled, attempting not to add to the heavy sadness in the room. Barbara and Maria both worked to regain their composure after several minutes.

"Okay, Maria. You win. How can I say no to this? Harold, what are the funeral arrangements?"

"We are having the service at Malibu Presbyterian Church. Tom will speak first, then myself, and finally Joshua will deliver a message."

"That's perfect. I knew I could rely on you, Son. Now, everybody out except Maria. We have to make sure this dress fits me just right before tomorrow."

Harold and Joshua left Maria behind and closed the door. Harold headed for his room, and Joshua went out on the sundeck in the backyard. The news in the last twenty-four hours had changed some things. However, he still was not sure what to think. Richard was desperate but not that desperate.

Why didn't he come to talk to me before he shot himself? Joshua stretched his legs out in front of him and stared at the distant ocean. *Sure, there is something going on with John, Jerry, and Trey, but Richard never said a word to me. Maybe Richard didn't think I would understand his problem? Maybe he thought I would be able to explain his suicide? That doesn't make sense. Why would anyone think anybody could understand suicide? There can be only one of two answers. Either Richard was hiding a terrible secret, a secret he kept so deeply hidden even I couldn't pick up on it, or the men Richard told Harry to pursue manipulated him until he felt he had no choice but to take his own life.*

Joshua stared out down the hill, past the other homes to the ocean below. The waves rolled in toward the cliffs of Malibu. Day in and day out, they always reacted the same way. Big waves, little waves, it did not matter. They always ended up crashing against the cliffs. *Why was life so unpredictable? Psychiatry was supposed to find the patterns of human behavior.*

Are there really patterns or do people all act randomly and science prefers to fool itself into believing there are patterns?

He heard a door open behind him. Joshua turned and saw Maria emerge with a rag and begin wiping down the chairs.

"Maria, I don't think the deck furniture is dirty."

Maria cocked her hand on her hip. "What do you know? You are a man who sits behind a desk, not the housekeeper."

Joshua knew Maria was joking, but her words wounded him just the same. Could he not even recognize dirt?

Maria dropped her hand, walked over, sat down next to Joshua, and took his hand. "I'm sorry, Joshua. I was just kidding. I can see you are upset."

Joshua wrapped both his hands around hers and spoke. "It isn't your fault."

Maria took her other hand and gently stroked the outside of his. Joshua looked down at their hands wrapped around one another. He had no desire to ever let go.

"Maria, do you know why Richard killed himself?"

Maria continued to hold his hands and looked him in his eyes as she spoke. "No. I don't like to think about that. Mr. Richard was one of the best men I have known. Other than you, of course."

Joshua shook his head. "I'm not feeling much like a good man. I don't know why Richard didn't come to me before killing himself. If I can't be trusted in somebody's hour of need, how can I be a good friend or psychiatrist?"

Maria gently rubbed his arm. "I don't think it was your fault or Richard's. We lived near Guadalajara when I was a young girl. My uncle had a store. These bad men would always come once a week and take his money. If he didn't hide some, they would take all of it. This went on for a couple of years. The police would not help because the bad men paid them. One day when I was in the store, the men came, and my uncle did not have as much money as he normally would. They said they would be back the next day, and if he did not have more money, they would take the store and me.

"My uncle was so upset. He cried and cried. He told my father what had happened. My father was afraid. These men were very powerful, and he could not stop them. That night, my uncle came over and I saw him give my father a lot of money. My father took my mother and me. I had nothing except my two dolls. The last I saw of my uncle, he was standing at the front door waving goodbye. We were just out of sight of our house when I heard a gunshot. I knew my uncle had taken his own life. I cried and cried. I loved my uncle very much. My dad explained to me that the bad men would not bother us because they would not find us with my uncle dead."

"Is that how you ended up here?"

"Eventually. My uncle didn't think the men would know about the money he had hidden, but they did. They had men everywhere. My parents sneaked over the border to get away from them when I was still a young girl. They were afraid to put me in school since we were not here legally. I was not able to learn like the other children. When Richard and Barbara moved here, they met our family through a friend who cleaned for the Richmonds. My mother was too old to do this work, but I was already cleaning other homes. Richard offered to help educate me, give me a full-time job and a place to live, and told my parents he would take care of them, as well. After my parents died, I stayed here because Richard and Barbara are like my family."

"So you think Richard is like your uncle?"

"Yes."

"But your uncle's plan didn't work out as he had hoped."

"That is true, but maybe God wanted us here. Maybe he wanted me to live with the Browns and maybe even meet you."

Maria's face turned slightly red, and she turned away for a moment.

Joshua felt warm inside. Almost alive again. Her hand had stopped stroking his arm. She held his hand in both of hers. They felt firm but so kind. He wanted to believe her words. That Richard had sacrificed himself to give the family time to escape whatever was coming. He was not a child though. Richard still should have come to him and talked through it.

Maria turned back and looked Joshua straight in the eyes. "Joshua, you are a good man, but you are not God. You can't know what Mr. Richard was thinking when he died. You may think you could have stopped him, but you could not. Even my father could not stop his brother. We all make up our own minds." She gave his hand a gentle squeeze and leaned forward to kiss his forehead. "I know you are a good man. Don't forget that."

Joshua could not deny the excitement of her lips on his forehead or her brushing past him to go back inside the house. What was it about Maria that suddenly had him so enamored? They had been around each other for eighteen years, and not once had he considered her in this way. They were both younger and better-looking years ago. Why not then? The small voice in the back of his mind responded, *Your job was your mistress.*

Harold strolled out on to the deck and sat down next to Joshua.

"Did Maria tell you what she did?"

Joshua gave him a confused look. "I don't think so."

Harold smiled and filled him in. "After we left, I heard the two of them in there laughing. At first, I was happy to hear Mom laughing again, but the giggling went on for a few minutes. I finally had to check and see what was going on. I knocked, and they got real quiet. I went in, and there's my mom in her regular clothes. I asked if she had already tried on her dress. She tells me she designed it. It turns out Maria told her what I was up to."

Joshua's lip curled up to the right and formed a half-smile. He spoke as much to himself as Harold. "Maria can be a sneaky one. So, what has your mom been up to? She stayed in her room for the last five days."

"Evidently, she knew Dad's password. That shouldn't surprise me, but I guess I thought she didn't care about the business. When we were sleeping, she was looking through the same documents we were. I didn't tell her about Darla. I don't think Mom needs to be in the middle of this. We don't know what we are going to find."

Joshua nodded. "How is she handling it? She may be giggling, and she may be investigating the laptop, but she isn't sleeping either."

"I know. Mom still looks a little frail, but she looks better than the first day. I hope going through Dad's stuff will keep her occupied."

Joshua shrugged. "Okay. It's not like we can do anything about it now. I take it the dress fits okay, then."

"Like a glove. At least that's what Mom told me."

That evening, Tom came over for dinner, and the three of them walked through the funeral. Barbara walked in and surprised the group. She wanted to make sure everything was in order. Joshua excused himself early and went into his office to contemplate his eulogy one last time.

He was at an impasse. How could he stand at the podium and talk about love, life, and sacrifice? Suicide was always the easiest answer. Anyone could quit. To honor his friend and ignore the anguish he left behind seemed disingenuous. Joshua decided to start typing and see what came out.

What can we say about a man who would give everything for his family? Very few men feel that depth of love. Yet even in our deepest love and compassion, we can sometimes make decisions that in the long run are mistakes. Fortunately, we have a savior whose grace covers our failings.

The words began to flow. Joshua could feel the darkness turn to gray. He did not have all the answers, but he would be able to honor his good friend and offer hope to the family. Joshua took the printed copy and slid it into his folder for the morning. He walked out and was surprised to find the house dark. The three hours he had spent focused on his speech had flown by. At least he understood why his eyes were so tired. Joshua quietly walked to his bedroom. He would need to talk to Maria about getting his house back tomorrow.

Chapter 5

Harold, Joshua, and Tom all sat drinking coffee and reading their notes. The driver would be there to pick up the family in an hour. Maria was assisting Barbara with her dress. Harold appeared to be counting in the air.

"Tom, the church is not that large. You are sure the extended family has seats?"

"Yes. Most of the seating is reserved, and there are a few back rows for guests. Don't worry about it, Harold. I'm sure everything is fine. How are you holding up?"

Harold stopped his air mathematics and looked at Tom. He spoke in a voice strained by grief. "Tom, we've been friends for a long time. You are like the brother I never had. I'm not doing that great, but I can get through this. How about you?"

Tom reached over and squeezed Harold's large forearm. "You know how much I love you and the whole family. My words can't express the pain I'm feeling right now, but we can get through this together."

Harold looked over at Joshua. "What about you, Doc? How are you holding up?"

Joshua thought for a long moment before responding. "As well as can be expected. I just hope I can honor Richard properly today."

"Doc, you were still typing when I went to bed. Is your eulogy ready?"

Joshua nodded his head. "Yes. Hopefully, I can keep some people awake."

Harold looked at his watch. "We have a half an hour. Where are those ladies?"

Maria and Barbara came walking out. The atmosphere changed in an instant. Barbara's dress was stunning and heartbreaking. All three men stood and began to tear up. Maria walked next to Barbara, all her mascara already cried away.

Harold spoke softly, "Is there anything I can get you, Mom?"

"No, Son. I'm glad you're here with me. Your father would be so proud of you these past few days."

Joshua reached out and gently took Barbara's hand. "Tom, Maria, and I will go wait for the car. We'll let you and Harold have some time alone."

Barbara responded in a hushed voice. "Thank you, Joshua."

Joshua walked out front. Tom and Maria followed. They stood in the small plaza near the entrance gate, waiting for the car. Joshua noticed the blooming cactus and thought how they felt out of place this day. Maria rested her head on Joshua's shoulder and gently cried. He put his arm around her and held her close. Tom walked a few steps away and read over his eulogy again.

Joshua was not sure what he was feeling. He was angry, still blaming himself for contributing to

Richard's death. *I just don't seem to be as invested in other's people's lives as I thought. Richard is gone, and yet I have no clue what drove him to it. Barbara has been snooping around every night, and I did not pick up on it. I can notice an officer's badge number and name but not a change in location for a laptop?*

Then there was Maria. *Maria, if you only knew the thoughts in my head now, you would blush and step away. They should not be here in this time and place, but you bring me such joy. Your luscious, thick black hair. Your curves, which you have maintained no matter what your age. The smell of your perfume and the sound of your voice. They feel like light and life to the heart and eyes of a man dying in despair.*

As if she had telepathy, Maria spoke. "It's okay, Joshua. You're a good man. I'm here for you."

He felt her arms wrap around his waist and hold him close. There was something safe in her five-foot-five frame. Tears began to drip down his cheeks. Joshua lost track of everything in that moment until he heard the car turning into the circular driveway. Maria released him and went inside to get Harold and Barbara.

Harold helped his mother into the limousine, and the others followed. Barbara looked at Tom and Harold.

"Neither of you invited those three awful men to the funeral, did you?"

"No, ma'am!" they responded in unison.

"Good. I couldn't stand to see their faces now."

She got inside the car.

The black limousine left the property for its winding drive through the hills to the church. They pulled up to a side door of the church and the family entered the building, walked a short distance down the small hallway, and were ushered into a private room. Barbara began to quietly weep again. Harold gently held her, and Tom left with the funeral director to get everything in place. Maria held a handkerchief in her left hand and Joshua's hand in her right. Joshua could only squeeze her hand in return. He had no answers for this day.

Tom walked back in. "It's time. Please follow me."

Barbara put her arm through Harold's, and the two of them followed Tom. Maria took Joshua's arm and followed. The sanctuary was overflowing. The pews were full; people lined the wall and had started to spill out into the foyer. Joshua could see through the opened doors more people coming in. Organ music played a somber tune. Tom showed Harold and his mother to the front pew. Maria sat between Harold and Joshua, and Tom sat next to Joshua. The front of the church held Richard's closed casket, draped in roses. It was a beautiful oak and brass coffin with hand-carved designs on the sides. To the left stood a large photo of the family, including Joshua and Tom. All of them wept as they took in the scene.

The organ finally stopped. Tom stood up and Joshua noticed his papers shaking slightly. He went up to the podium and began to speak. "Today we mourn a man who gave so much to so many. Each of us here benefited from his wisdom, his friendship, and even his business sense. I remember spending my childhood over at the Browns'. Richard taught Harold and me the joys of football, baseball, and swimming. Harold and I would come back from our hiking adventures in the hills, and Richard would always want to hear everything we experienced. He made us feel like world travelers."

Joshua's mind wandered while Tom spoke. He remembered Richard telling him he came all the way across the country to North Carolina to find a son and then returned to find his savior. Joshua had scolded him for the second comment, but Richard just laughed.

"Joshua, you are a rare find. A man of conviction. If anyone can help my son, and maybe even our whole family, it's you. Name your price."

Now here they were at his funeral after he shot himself in the head. A voice hissed inside his head. *You haven't saved anybody. Harold still can't function on his own. The family is codependent—not free individuals who can think for themselves.* He heard the rustling of paper and felt the pew creak as Harold pushed himself up. Harold began his slow walk toward the podium. His head drooped down and shoulders slunk forward, the weight of his grief displayed to the entire church.

Tom walked down, and they hugged one another. Tom whispered something to Harold, and they hugged again. Harold walked up. He shuffled with his papers and wiped his eyes. He stopped, took in a deep breath, and began to speak. "Many of you knew my father, but I was the only person who knew him as Dad. He was a man of strong convictions. He made sure I became the same sort of man."

Harold stopped and stared. Joshua looked over his shoulder to see what had caught Harold's attention. Senator Trey Jones sat in the middle of a pew in the center section, along with Richmond and Guilford.

He saw Harold's face begin to turn red. Harold closed his eyes and took a deep breath.

"As I was saying, my father was a man of great convictions. Convictions he put deep inside of me. He was a man who put everyone before himself, especially those who worked for him. He loved you all. Unfortunately, he could not live with the knowledge that men who were not like him, men with no scruples, men with no conscience, men like Senator Trey Jones, John Richmond, and Jerry Guilford, who would seek to destroy both our company and our family."

The senator stood up and yelled, "That's a dirty rotten lie!"

Harold was undeterred. "No, Senator, the only one rotten here is you and your two cronies. Stand up, you three. Let everyone see who caused my father's death. His blood is on your hands!"

Barbara stood up and pointed her finger at the three men. "Get out of here! Isn't it enough you try to bankrupt us? Now you try and destroy our hope? You destroyed my husband! Have you no self-respect?"

Harold started down from the stage, but Joshua intervened.

"Get out of my way, Doc."

Joshua responded in a hushed tone below the chatter behind him. "Not this way, Harry. You can't save your mom or the company this way. Don't let them take the legacy of your father too."

Harold looked at Tom and roared, "Get that trash out of here!"

Before Tom could move, a Parabolic board member and a distant relative each had a CEO by the arm and were roughly dragging them into the aisle. The senator retreated quickly on his own. Barbara burst into tears and then grabbed the pew.

Joshua knew the signs and yelled at Harold, "Dial 911. Your mom is having a heart attack!"

Barbara collapsed into Joshua's arms, and he laid her on the ground. There was no pulse, and he immediately started CPR.

Harold ran over. "Mom!"

"Harold, did you make the call?"

"Yes!" came from Harold and about twenty other people behind them.

Tom worked to get the crowd back so Barbara could have some air and privacy. Maria held Barbara's hand and prayed. The EMTs arrived and began to work on Barbara. A faint pulse returned. Joshua got in the back of the ambulance with Barbara, and Harold got into the passenger seat. The ambulance sped away toward St. John's Regional Medical Center. Joshua and the EMT worked constantly to start Barbara's heart. Sweat dripped from their faces and Joshua screamed at both the driver and his partner to hurry up and try harder. Joshua looked down at his watch as the ambulance made the turn into the hospital's emergency entrance, They had been beating, shocking, and massaging Barbara's still heart for thirty minutes.

Joshua's tear-soaked face met Harold's when the rear doors opened.

The EMT sitting across from him said, "I'm so sorry."

Harold let out a roar, and everything stopped in place. Then he passed out and hit the ground. The EMTs and nurses rushed over. He was breathing. I trauma team took Barbara's lifeless body into the hospital in one last futile attempt to revive her. Six medical personnel worked to get Harold's large body onto a gurney. They rolled him into a trauma room and began to check his vitals.

A doctor walked up to Joshua and introduce himself. "I'm Dr. Gutierrez. I understand this man's mother died on the way to the hospital. Can you please help me understand what happened?"

Joshua introduced himself as the family psychiatrist. He gave Dr. Gutierrez the information he needed. Joshua avoided giving anymore details than necessary. He needed to protect Harold, and the family's reputation.

Gutierrez took down Joshua's information and said, "As the family psychiatrist, you are welcome to take over the case, of course. I do have office hours outside the hospital and will be happy to assist in any way you see fit."

What Joshua really wanted to do was crawl into a cave and never see anyone or anything of this world again, but he knew that was not an option.

"Thank you. I'm not sure I'm able to do that now. Please remain on his case."

"We'll sedate Mr. Brown for the next two days. Hopefully, that will give his brain time to process what has happened without harming his mind. Do you need anything?"

"Just some alone time myself. The family and I were very close. Seeing you have the situation in hand here removes some of the burden. One word of advice: Harold tends to be resilient. Please have the nurses monitor him and adjust the doses higher, if you need to."

"Thank you, Dr. Zeev. I will make a note of it."

"Here is my card. Please call me if there is a problem or when you plan to wake him up."

"Thank you. I'm sorry for your loss, Doctor."

"Thank you, so am I."

Joshua walked out of the emergency room and into the waiting room. Tom had a look of shock, and Maria was in a corner crying. Joshua knew they had received the official news that Barbara had passed away. Maria saw Joshua and ran up to him. They put their arms around one another and cried. The waiting room melted away from Joshua's view. All he saw was Maria. He closed his eyes and imagined the two of them alone in a cave, safe from the world and all its pain. Maria released him, and the hospital waiting room came rushing back into view.

Joshua took a step back and Tom asked, "They said at the desk Harold collapsed. Is he okay?"

Joshua wiped the tears from his cheeks. "Hopefully he will be. A Dr. Gutierrez is handling it. He's going to help Harold relax for a couple of days."

"I know what has happened!" Maria exclaimed with a frown. "Those awful men upset Miss Barbara, and now she is dead."

Tom nodded his head in agreement.

Joshua also nodded slightly. "They probably helped. Barbara already had a broken heart. Her nighttime sleuthing just helped keep her mind off it. In her fragile state, those men appearing at the funeral was more than Barbara's fragile body could handle."

"You are being too nice, Joshua." Maria scowled at him. "A funeral should be about love and family. Those men had no business being there."

Tom chimed in. "She's right. Why were they there?"

The thought had not occurred to Joshua. "That's a good question. Harold has someone looking at them. Maybe she will come back with something."

Joshua could see he had piqued Tom's interest. "Who is she?"

Joshua thought better about sharing too much information. "I imagine Harry will tell you when he is feeling better. Anything he and I discuss is considered confidential unless he tells me differently."

Tom shook his head. "Of course, Doctor. I'm sorry."

Joshua reached out and squeezed Tom's shoulder. "It's okay. Did you ride with Maria?"

"No, I brought my own car."

Joshua put his arm around Maria. Her firm, warm body brought strength to his spent soul. "Would you mind staying and getting me the details from the hospital about Barbara's body? I really want to get home. Today has been very trying."

Tom looked at Joshua and Maria holding one another. "Of course, Doctor. I assume Maria will take you back?"

"Yes. Unless there is a problem, please plan on coming by my house tomorrow."

Tom shook hands with both. "Okay. I hope things get better."

"Don't we all."

Maria took Joshua's hand and walked him out to her car. They left the hospital, and she reached over and held his hand again all the way home. Joshua looked out the front window and saw nothing. His entire existence just seemed to be a void. He wanted to go hide in his sanctuary.

"Maria, I hate to ask, but would it be possible to have my house back tonight? I really need to be in my home right now."

Maria squeezed his hand as if she understood his real meaning. "That's fine. I miss my room. I can move my things out shortly."

The beautiful coastline that normally brought a smile to Joshua now passed by unnoticed. He just wanted to hide away from the world. "No, just leave them there. We've both been through so much. Are you okay with me leaving my things until tomorrow?"

"Of course, Joshua. Leave them as long as you like."

He continued to hold her hand as they traveled. The thought of having Maria beside him was more appealing than being alone.

"Would you like to come up and sit on my porch with me? I could really use your company, as well as the view."

She gave his hand a firm squeeze. "I would love to."

Maria parked her car at the estate, and the two of them crossed the road and made the short walk to his house. He let go of Maria's hand and collapsed in his favorite rocking chair. Joshua stared over the estate and the ocean below. He wondered if his pain and guilt would ever go away. To his side, he heard the scraping of wood. He looked over and saw Maria finish dragging her rocking chair close to his. She held his arm with both her hands and put her head on his shoulder. Joshua rested his head on hers. A faint glimmer of hope pierced into the darkness.

Chapter 6

The cell phone rang next to Joshua's bed. He rolled over, and the large digital display read 9:00 a.m. He grabbed the phone, if only to stop the ringing.

"Hello, this is Dr. Zeev."

"Doctor, this is Dr. Gutierrez. I wanted to let you know we had a problem with Harold."

The fog immediately left Joshua's head and he sat up. "What sort of problem?"

"Mr. Brown began thrashing about in his sleep last night. At one point, he yelled so loudly it woke up the entire floor. It took four nurses to hold him down. We have restrained him for his own safety."

Joshua sat up on the edge of the bed. "Is he awake?"

"No. It appears to have been some strange nightmare. Something even manifested physically."

Joshua rubbed the front of his face and slapped his cheeks to ensure he was fully alert. "What do you mean?"

"A shallow two-inch cut appeared on his chest. It looks like a scalpel or sharp knife cut him."

A physical cut from a dream? Did he need to be involved more? "Is it possible he cut himself when he was flailing about?"

"It's possible. Although the cut is so clean it seems improbable."

"How many episodes did he have?"

"He had two. We increased his medicine by ten percent each time, and now he is finally quiet."

Joshua had never seen Harold experience any sort of rage in his sleep. A fearful thought ran through his mind. *Is Harry's mind breaking? Maybe my last session did more harm than good? I better make sure he stays asleep to give his mind a chance to bounce back.*

"I would leave him on that dose then. Unless something else happens, I think we can leave him sedated as you originally planned."

"I agree. I am actually hesitant to wake him up if he is that agitated in his sleep."

Joshua stood up and paced his room. "Please do me one favor, Doctor. Call me so I can be there when you wake him up." Then an idea occurred to Joshua. "Doctor, what do you think about sending Harry to Avalon Malibu? They have an excellent mental health facility."

"What sort of timeline are you thinking about, Doctor?"

Joshua had to think. He did not want Harold to wake up and find himself locked away. He might try and check himself out—or worse, just leave.

"Let me speak to him, and then I can give you my timeline. In the meantime, would you mind calling Avalon and planning for his arrival? Just tell them it may be as long as two weeks."

"Absolutely," responded Dr. Gutierrez.

"Thank you. Have a good morning."

Joshua hung up the phone. He felt helpless. Everything he had touched for the last eighteen years seemed to be falling apart. If Harold was having a mental breakdown, Joshua would have to help him. Except he felt as if he were the last person who should help. His self-pity attempted to convict him once more. *You know this all started with Richard. Do you really think the two of you were that tight? Do you think Harry is close to you? Is he close like Richard? Are you ready for another casket?*

Joshua sat there, fighting his own depression. A smell like lilacs caught his attention. He looked around his room, but nobody was there, and there were no flowers. He recognized the smell—Maria's perfume. She must have stayed in his bed when she was in his house. Why would she have done that when she had her own room?

The perfume drew him in. He grabbed the extra pillow and inhaled. His eyes closed, and he could still feel her goodnight hug. Something inside him stirred, the room fell away, and Joshua could see himself in a field of flowers. He never wanted to leave, but he knew he had to.

He got off the bed, showered, and grabbed a late morning coffee. As much as he loathed to do it, he took the sheets off the bed and threw them into the washer. After walking into his television room, he stopped. What had happened? Black lace and fabric lay everywhere. He didn't remember the mess being there last night, but he had gone straight to bed after Maria said goodnight on the front porch. He had no idea making a dress could be so expansive. His doorbell rang.

Joshua looked up at the ceiling and said, "Of course, someone is at the door now."

Joshua gave an annoyed huff and walked to the front door. Maria stood there in a black Spanish skirt and white ruffled blouse. Her hair was down. She had his suitcase with her.

"I thought I would help you out."

Joshua smiled. "You look lovely. Please come in."

"Thank you. With nobody in the house, there is little cleaning to do today. I thought I would put on something a little nicer. I'm glad you like it. Do you mind if I pick up the things from my little sewing project?"

Joshua laughed. "Little? I would hate to see large."

Maria put down the suitcase. "Oh, you should see five ladies sewing together. When I was a little girl in my village, the women would get together and make clothes."

Joshua tried to imagine Maria as a young girl, laughing and playing in her small village.

"That must have been something to see."

Maria had a gleam in her eye. "It was."

Joshua picked up his suitcase and walked it to the laundry room off the kitchen as he spoke over his shoulder. "I can help you, if you'd like."

Maria followed. "You let me use your house. I would not think of imposing more."

Joshua dropped the suitcase just inside the laundry room and turned around. "It's no imposition. I would love to help you."

He started to ask himself what he was thinking and threw it out of his mind. He did not care anymore. She was the one person who made him feel human. When he was around Maria, he felt like he could forgive his own faults. She seemed to like him despite his failings, so why couldn't he? It felt as if no time had passed before she was ready to go back to the main house with her equipment.

"I can help you take those back."

Joshua failed at trying to hide his eagerness.

Maria stood there. Her arms filled with her sewing machine and bits of fabric large and small. Her dark eyes barely peered over the black lace. "I would like that, but I need to get some shopping done. Harold comes back tomorrow, and he is a big eater."

"Please, come sit for just a moment then."

Maria followed Joshua to the living room. She put down her bounty and sat next to him on the couch.

He turned to her and said, "Maria, Harry is going to be moved to Avalon. It's a mental health rehabilitation facility here in Malibu."

Tears began to fill Maria's eyes. She buried her head into Joshua's shoulder.

"Is Harold crazy?"

Joshua held her and shook his head. "No, nothing like that. He has been through so much. I just want Harry to have some peace and quiet. Coming directly home will only bring everything rushing back to him."

Maria sat up and wiped her eyes with a tissue from her pocket. "So, Harold will be okay?"

Joshua smiled and held her hand between his. "I'm positive he will be okay. Harry's going to be better than okay."

Maria smiled and put her tissue away. "You see, Joshua, you are a good man and a good doctor. I still need to go shopping though. We need to eat too."

"That's true. We don't want to be hungry."

They both laughed.

Maria expertly picked up her load of materials and sewing machine and walked back across the road to the estate. Joshua stood on his porch, and for the first time didn't see the blue Pacific stretched out before him. Smiling, he came back inside and sat in the recliner in his entertainment room.

He started to grab the remote and stopped himself. What was he thinking? *We both like each other. At least it seems that way, but she's ten years younger. She's part of the family. If Harry is like a son I never had, what does that make Maria?* A smile came across Joshua's face. *The housekeeper.* He shook his head. *No, that wasn't funny. She isn't some doll for me to play with while I'm sad. I need to figure out what is going on.*

He pulled his phone from his pocket and dialed.

"Dr. Adam."

Joshua could not hide the edge in his voice. "Adam, Joshua. I hope I'm not interrupting anything."

Adam's calm southern drawl soothed Joshua's conflicted soul. "Just paperwork. You never call my personal number. This must be really important."

Joshua began pacing his living room. "I'm not sure where to start. First, Barbara has passed away. It appeared to be a heart attack."

"Good Lord! I am so sorry to hear that. How did Harold take it?"

"He collapsed and is in the hospital. I think he'll be okay. I'm having him moved to a mental health rehab center here in Malibu for a couple of weeks. That will give his mind and body time to adjust to his new reality before having to face it."

Adam's tone and tenor rose as he grasped the seriousness of everything happening. "What can I do to help?"

Joshua walked out of the living room and began to pace in his great room. "I'm not sure. I seem to be doubting myself more and more, but it gets worse."

"Oh, my goodness! What is worse?" Joshua heard the squeak Adam's chair made when he would stand up in a hurry.

Joshua stopped and looked out his sliding glass door into his backyard. "Do you remember me mentioning our housekeeper, Maria?"

"Yes, the young Latin woman and her family that Richard helped before you moved in. Don't tell me she is in the hospital too."

Joshua looked down at the floor. "If only it were that easy. I think we may be falling for each other."

"As in falling in love? Or tripping over one another?"

Joshua could almost hear Adam's chuckle in the question.

He began swinging his free arm around in exaggerated gestures to nobody in the room. "I'm being serious,

Adam. I have been here eighteen years. Why now? I'm concerned all these crises are pushing us together. I don't want to hurt her. To be honest, I don't want to be hurt."

"As a peer, let me give you my professional opinion. I'm surprised it has taken you fifty-eight years to acknowledge you are actually a real man and not just a psychiatrist."

Joshua stopped his flailing and bowed his head in defeat. "I'm not sure you are helping me."

Adam's voice was smooth and slow. "Listen, Joshua, as your friend, take my advice. Don't fight it. Sit down with Maria and ask her why she has her feelings. If she acknowledges she is lonely and scared because of these deaths, then yes, you should stop what is happening. If not, perhaps you should pursue it. Isn't she ten years younger than you?"

"Yes."

"Mazel tov!"

Joshua sat down in an empty dining room chair. He did not have the energy to argue. "Okay. I hear what you are saying. Yes, she is an attractive woman. She is young but not too young. If this were any other time, I would only be calling to celebrate. You win. I'll follow your advice."

"Good. Let me know how it turns out. I am praying for you all out there. Now, tell me more about Harold."

Joshua paused for a moment and crossed his arms to help him focus. "He had an episode while he was sedated. It almost sounded like one of our sessions. His arms were flailing about, and he even got cut during the incident."

"Perhaps his brain is trying to tap into subconscious memories to deal with all that has happened."

Joshua rubbed his furrowed brow. "Maybe. They increased the sedation. We'll see what happens when he wakes up tomorrow. In the meantime, I'll follow your so-called advice about Maria. I'll update you on everything when I can."

"Please do."

Joshua hung up. At least it was Sunday. He could lose himself to football for the remainder of the day. He needed the rest. Joshua picked up the remote and tuned into the pregame show on Fox.

The doorbell woke him up. The second game was already on. Joshua got up and answered the door.

Maria stood there with a basket full of food. "I'm not used to cooking for just myself. I thought we could share some dinner together."

Joshua smiled. He loved the offer. "That sounds like a great idea. Do you want to eat on the porch? We can enjoy the view together."

Maria looked over her shoulder and returned her gaze to Joshua. "I would enjoy that very much."

She had brought cheese, fruit, wine, and herb chicken. He grabbed a couple of small tables on the porch and set them in front of two chairs. Maria prepared the plates and put the basket between the chairs with the wine bottle and some extra fruit inside.

Joshua noticed the bottle was one of the nicer labels kept in the estate's wine cellar. "Where did you get your taste in wine?"

Maria grinned. "I learned from watching the Browns pick their wines for dinner."

"You're a quick study."

"Thank you."

The events over the last week had left their diet sketchy at best. Both their bodies craved the fresh food. They ate in silence for a few minutes. Joshua finished his chicken and reached into the basket for a fresh plump strawberry. He sat up.

"Maria, I have a question. A serious question."

Maria quickly finished chewing and stared deeply into his eyes. "Of course, Joshua. You can ask me anything."

Joshua finished his strawberry, trying to buy time to find the right words. "It seems we have gotten a lot closer this week since Richard's death."

Maria gave him a shy smile, looked down, and spoke softly. "Yes, I know."

He took his finger and gently lifted her chin, so they were looking eye to eye again. "I'm just curious as to why. We have known each other eighteen years."

Maria gave him a confused look. "Why does that matter?"

Joshua looked deeply into her beautiful, confused eyes. "I'm concerned we might be getting closer because we are both hurting. I know I feel very lonely and empty, except when you're around."

Maria sat up in her chair. "Joshua, you mean you really don't know?"

He shook his head slowly. "I'm afraid I don't."

Maria scowled and shook her head in frustration. "Why are smart men always so stupid?"

She stopped. Her gaze felt as if it were penetrating the deepest parts of Joshua's heart, and then she continued, "I have cared for you since you first moved in. I didn't bother you because you were here to help Harold. I didn't want to get in the way of your work. I wanted Harold cured. Then Richard set up your blog. I heard you and Richard talking about the people you helped. You were both so happy with your work."

Joshua took her hand. "If I had known … I mean, I just never noticed, I guess."

She shook her head. "You had your work. That was your world. This week, for the first time, you looked different. You were hurting. You looked lonely and lost. I knew I could help you. Then you noticed me as a woman. I have waited eighteen years for that."

Joshua looked up at the ceiling of the covered patio. "Have I been that tied up in my work all these years?"

She took his hands. "I would not call it tied up. You helped Harold so much. Your love for him is obvious. Before you came, the Browns could not control him when he had his fits. If you had not helped, they would have had to put him in a hospital. Now he is a man. I know he breaks things, but not like he used to."

Joshua's head drooped. "I wanted to cure him."

Maria lifted his chin, so he had to look at her. "He has his freedom, doesn't he? He is going to take over his father's company. He is cured enough."

Joshua leaned closer to Maria. "When I look in your eyes, I believe you. When you leave, though, all my doubts and condemnation return. The Browns' estate condemns me. I still see Richard's brains on the wall in his office. I'm sorry. I shouldn't be so graphic."

"You're a quick study."

"Thank you."

The events over the last week had left their diet sketchy at best. Both their bodies craved the fresh food. They ate in silence for a few minutes. Joshua finished his chicken and reached into the basket for a fresh plump strawberry. He sat up.

"Maria, I have a question. A serious question."

Maria quickly finished chewing and stared deeply into his eyes. "Of course, Joshua. You can ask me anything."

Joshua finished his strawberry, trying to buy time to find the right words. "It seems we have gotten a lot closer this week since Richard's death."

Maria gave him a shy smile, looked down, and spoke softly. "Yes, I know."

He took his finger and gently lifted her chin, so they were looking eye to eye again. "I'm just curious as to why. We have known each other eighteen years."

Maria gave him a confused look. "Why does that matter?"

Joshua looked deeply into her beautiful, confused eyes. "I'm concerned we might be getting closer because we are both hurting. I know I feel very lonely and empty, except when you're around."

Maria sat up in her chair. "Joshua, you mean you really don't know?"

He shook his head slowly. "I'm afraid I don't."

Maria scowled and shook her head in frustration. "Why are smart men always so stupid?"

She stopped. Her gaze felt as if it were penetrating the deepest parts of Joshua's heart, and then she continued, "I have cared for you since you first moved in. I didn't bother you because you were here to help Harold. I didn't want to get in the way of your work. I wanted Harold cured. Then Richard set up your blog. I heard you and Richard talking about the people you helped. You were both so happy with your work."

Joshua took her hand. "If I had known … I mean, I just never noticed, I guess."

She shook her head. "You had your work. That was your world. This week, for the first time, you looked different. You were hurting. You looked lonely and lost. I knew I could help you. Then you noticed me as a woman. I have waited eighteen years for that."

Joshua looked up at the ceiling of the covered patio. "Have I been that tied up in my work all these years?"

She took his hands. "I would not call it tied up. You helped Harold so much. Your love for him is obvious. Before you came, the Browns could not control him when he had his fits. If you had not helped, they would have had to put him in a hospital. Now he is a man. I know he breaks things, but not like he used to."

Joshua's head drooped. "I wanted to cure him."

Maria lifted his chin, so he had to look at her. "He has his freedom, doesn't he? He is going to take over his father's company. He is cured enough."

Joshua leaned closer to Maria. "When I look in your eyes, I believe you. When you leave, though, all my doubts and condemnation return. The Browns' estate condemns me. I still see Richard's brains on the wall in his office. I'm sorry. I shouldn't be so graphic."

Maria pulled his hand to her chest. "Joshua. You must forgive yourself."

Tears began to flow from his eyes. "I don't know if I can."

She held his hand firmly between her breasts. "I will be here for you. Believe me, you are a good man."

Maria leaned over and kissed his cheek. Joshua felt a spark rush through his body. He wanted to believe everything she said. Maria gently pulled his hand away.

"I should go back to the house. I need to get dinner cleaned up."

Joshua's body felt like it had he had just dropped a two-hundred-pound sack off his back. Although he was exhausted, he wanted to help Maria.

"Would you like some help?"

She reached over and placed her soft hand on his shoulder. "You should rest."

Joshua gathered their trash, and Maria put the remains of their meal back in the basket. He grabbed the leftover wine. "Would you like me to take care of our leftovers? The wine should keep for a day or two. Perhaps you could drop back over for a sunset, and we can finish the bottle?"

She smiled and said, "That sounds perfect."

Maria handed Joshua the basket and held his gaze. Then with a sly grin, she turned on her heel and sauntered across the road back to the estate. Joshua wanted that moment to last forever.

Chapter 7

Joshua stood in the doorway and looked at Harold strapped in his bed by his wrists. The sleeping giant was at peace. He hoped Harold would remain so when they woke him up. A voice from behind startled him.

"Dr. Zeev, good morning," Dr. Gutierrez said.

Joshua turned around. "Good morning, Doctor. Has he had any more episodes?"

Dr. Gutierrez looked over the clipboard in his hand. "Not since we increased his sedation."

"That's good news. I would like the restraints removed before we wake him."

Dr. Gutierrez looked uneasy at the suggestion. "We were concerned what he might do as he wakes up."

Joshua shook his head. "Trust me. If he really wanted to be violent, those straps could not hold him. If it makes everyone feel better, why don't we bring him out of his sleep very slowly, and we can take the straps off right before he fully wakes?"

"That sounds reasonable, Doctor."

Dr. Gutierrez had a nurse come in and reduce his medication, and then the two of them left the room.

Joshua hoped Harold would not blame him for his mother's death. *I was the one who insisted she come to the funeral. If we had left Barbara in her room, I'm sure she would have eventually given up and died, but she seemed strong enough to handle the stress.* Joshua smiled to himself. *She really took on those three scumbags.* His smile faded to a frown. *Right up until she died. Nobody knew they would be there. In fact, they all agreed not to invite them. What about Harold? Did my eighteen years of hypnotherapy and counseling send his mind crashing in when real trouble came calling? I'm not sure I could forgive myself if I allowed my study of his condition to blind me to the young man I have claimed to love as a son.*

Dr. Gutierrez walked back into the room and checked the nurse's notes in the computer. Joshua squeezed Harold's large hand and looked up at the doctor.

"How long do we have before he starts waking up?"

Dr. Gutierrez logged out and turned to Joshua. "Close to two hours. You have time to grab some breakfast, if you'd like."

"Thank you. I'm going down to grab some coffee. Please call me if anything changes."

"Absolutely."

Joshua walked down to the elevator and pressed the lobby button. *Why am I beating myself up? I wasn't involved with the funeral. Of course, Harold won't blame me. He had Maria make his mother a dress to ensure she would go. I wasn't even involved in the decision.*

Grabbing his coffee, he sat down at a table and pulled out his cell phone to check his email. The phone's ringer went off with it resting in his palm.

"Dr. Zeev."

"Doctor, this is Darla."

Her voice sounded guarded. Joshua sat up on the edge of his chair.

"Darla, I didn't expect to hear from you. Please call me Joshua. Where are you?"

"I prefer not to say."

Joshua got up and moved over to an empty table by a window and faced it. "Oh, so you're back. Good. Did you find out anything?"

Darla's voice sounded a bit more monotone and lower than he remembered. "I'm in the field. It's worse than anyone can imagine. Do you still want to help me?"

His foot started to tap the floor. "Yes, what do I need to do?"

"Hold on a moment."

Joshua heard Darla put her phone against her clothes and then some muffled voices.

"Do you think he's interested?"

He could barely make out the voice, but it sounded like a man. Darla said something, and then there was a long silence. Joshua held his breath.

Darla returned, speaking more loudly. "As I was saying, Joshua, I can't wait to see you. I'm sorry to hear Harold has decided to evict you. I can assure you, the men I'm working with will reward you for your diligence."

Joshua drew in a breath. "I see. When do you want me there?"

"I will arrange a ticket for you to fly out in the morning. Expect to meet me upon your arrival at Key West. We will take a private plane to the island. Does that work for you?"

"Certainly."

Darla hung up. What could she possibly have found?

I need to fly out tomorrow? How am I going to get Harry to the hospital and have everything packed in time? I'm not a young man anymore. I need to go. Darla wouldn't call me if the answers were somewhere else. First things first: I need to take care of Harry.

Joshua got up and headed back up to Harold's room. He spoke to the empty elevator. "I should check Harry's cut before I leave."

The elevator doors opened, and he walked directly to the nurses' station.

"My name is Dr. Zeev. Do you know Dr. Gutierrez's location? He is treating a patient of mine, Harold Brown."

The nurse looked up from her computer. "I can page him."

Joshua tapped the counter as he talked. "Please do."

Dr. Gutierrez arrived a brief time later. "What is it, Dr. Zeev? Is something wrong?"

Joshua shook his head. "A thought occurred to me downstairs. You mentioned Harold was cut. I'm curious, how did you treat the cut?"

Dr. Gutierrez walked behind the nurse's station and started typing on an empty keyboard. "Let me see what is in the computer. Oh, yes, here it is. It was superficial. We just applied antibiotic cream and a simple bandage."

Joshua walked around to join the doctor. "There were no signs of discoloration around the wound?"

Dr. Gutierrez shook his head. "None. The flesh was perfectly sliced, no sign of irritation or tearing."

Joshua thought for a moment. *Thank goodness. After Darla's phone call, I was afraid somebody had tried to kill Harry. From the sounds of it, he probably cut it in his sleep, but on what? The wound sounds like a scalpel cut. That doesn't make any sense. There wouldn't be any knives of that type left lying around within reach of a patient. If it were an accident, where did that cut originate from?*

Dr. Gutierrez cleared his throat. "Dr. Zeev, is there anything else?"

Joshua shook his head. "I'm sorry, Doctor. How much longer before we can remove his straps?"

"We can remove the straps now, if you'd like."

Joshua agreed. Both doctors and the nurse headed to Harold's room to unstrap him. All three stood and stared at Harold's freed limbs. Would Harold sense the release and begin jerking around again? After two minutes of Harold breathing deeply, Dr. Gutierrez and the nurse left. Joshua pulled up a chair next to Harold and held his hand.

"Harry, I don't know if you can hear me yet. You've been through a lot in a brief period. I feel helpless in all of this. I don't know what I can offer at this point, but I am here for you."

"Doc, you need to quit beating yourself up." Harold gently squeezed Joshua's hand. He slowly opened his eyes and smiled. "I'm so glad you're here, Doc."

Joshua bent over, and the two men hugged. Joshua sat back. Harold looked at both his arms.

"Hey, Doc, why are there strap marks on my wrists?"

Joshua looked at Harold's wrists and turned them gently in his hands. "What do you remember?"

"I remember seeing Mom lying there."

Tears rolled down Harold's cheeks.

Joshua squeezed Harold's right arm. "I'm sorry, Harry. This can wait."

He wiped the tears from his cheeks "No, Doc, it might be a long wait. I remember waking up and seeing an IV in my arm. I guess I was a little upset. A nurse came up to my bed and said she was giving me something to help me relax. Then I woke up here."

Joshua pulled out a pocket notebook from his shirt and a pen. "Are you sure that's all you remember? Do you remember having a dream?"

Harold laid there staring at the ceiling. His forehead crinkled up and then a slight smile came across his face. "I did. I did, Doc. In fact, you were there."

Joshua sat up on the edge of his chair and began to take notes. "Interesting. What were you dreaming?"

"It was just like one of our sessions. I was the bear and you were the wolf. Then another wolf joined us. It was Bill. You know, my half-brother."

Joshua lowered his notepad. "Bill? Why would Bill be in your dream?"

He fell back against his chair. *What was happening to Harry?* Joshua chased pieces of thoughts that led nowhere.

Harold shrugged. "You're the psychiatrist, Doc. Anyway, we were telling him about Mom and Dad. We told him how Trey, John, and Jerry conspired to kill them."

Harold's last statement distracted Joshua. "Harry, why do you think they tried to kill your mother?"

Harold raised his bed, so he could look at Joshua easier. "Dad had that argument with John before his death. I think they went to the funeral to see what we might know and to maybe upset Mom."

Joshua noted Harold's theory in his notepad. "So you think they killed her?"

Harold's middle finger began lightly tapping the bed's guardrail. "I don't know if they meant to, but that was in my dream."

"Was there anything else in your dream?"

Joshua had scooted back up to the edge of his chair.

"Yeah, Doc. Do you want me to talk about my theories on my parents' murders or my dream?"

"Sorry, please continue about your dream."

Harold crossed his arms and rested their weight on his stomach. "Well, as I was saying, we were talking to Bill when out of the woods Trey, John, and Jerry appeared. The weird thing was they dressed like Viking warriors too. None of them ever said a word. They simply walked up with their shields raised, and the fight was on. You killed Trey with one thrust of your sword. Bill hacked off Jerry's head with a swift swing of his axe.

John was tougher than I thought. I swung my axe and hit him in the shoulder, but he cut me across my chest at the same time. He couldn't raise his axe again because of his shoulder, so I decapitated him."

Joshua shook his head. He reached over and felt the chest bandage through Harold's gown. "Harry, I need you to look at your chest."

Harold slapped at the bandage. "Why, Doc? Why is there a bandage there?"

"It's nothing serious. Here, let me show you."

Harold carefully raised his hospital gown under the sheet to expose his chest.

Joshua examined the wound under the bandage. There was no redness or infection. "Was the cut in your dream where that bandage is?"

Harold looked a little scared. "I'm not sure, Doc. I mean, it was a dream. That is weird. I mean, it could be. I don't remember exactly."

Joshua carefully peeled back the bandage. It was a clean, shallow cut. No tearing or ripping. He put the bandage back down in place.

"Don't worry, Harry. Dr. Gutierrez said you were flailing around in bed at one point. That is probably where the cut came from. The doctor tied you down so you wouldn't hurt yourself. Harry, you're sure about your dream?"

"I'm sure, Doc. I know because the three of us poured their blood into these mugs we had and drank it."

Joshua covered Harold back up. "I'm not normally one to drink the blood of my enemies, but anything is possible in a dream. Was there anything else?"

"I had a second dream. I didn't recognize the men we killed. They looked Mediterranean or something."

"Was Bill in that dream as well?"

"Yeah."

"I understand the first dream. I have a lot of hatred for these men too. They took your father from me as well. I'm not sure about your second dream. Perhaps it isn't related to anything."

Harold shook his head. "I don't know, Doc. Maybe it's all just a dream."

Joshua reached over and took Harold's hand. "You may be right. Harry, Dr. Gutierrez and I have been talking. We both agree you need to take some time to let your parents' deaths soak in. We think you need to get away for a bit."

Harold took back his hand and sat up straight. "Away! What do you mean? Like a vacation or something?"

Joshua slid back in his chair. "Something like that. We want you to go to a mental rehab center in Malibu named Avalon. It is more like a resort than a hospital. Dr. Gutierrez will come by every day and talk to you."

"And where are you going to be, Doc?"

Joshua leaned in. "I have to fly out of town. Darla says she needs my help in her investigation."

Harold attempted to get out of bed. "Then I'm going too!"

Joshua held up his arms. "Hold on, Harry. This is what I mean. You have not even mentioned your mother's death or her funeral. You're totally focused on taking these guys on instead. Can't you see? You're doing what your mother did. You're trying to hide from your grief by making yourself busy and distracted. However, your brain knows what is really going on. If you don't allow your mind time to deal with your losses, you could break it."

Harold laid back and quieted. "Do you mean, like a bone or something?"

"Yes, Harry, that is exactly what I mean. The brain is just an organ. When it's overstressed, it tries to adjust. Sometimes it can temporarily release chemicals to keep itself in balance. If the stress continues for too long or if it is too intense, it will become chemically imbalanced. We really don't understand much around the brain, but I know enough to tell you if that happens, there is no guarantee you will get better. Ignoring your mental health can be very dangerous."

Harold's face became solemn. "Like ignoring your heart and having a heart attack."

Joshua took his hand again. "Yes, that's an effective way to say it."

"Okay, Doc. You win. When do we go?"

Joshua patted Harold's hand and relaxed in his chair. "Dr. Gutierrez will make the arrangements. I imagine sometime today. Maria will come visit until I get back."

"How long will you be gone?"

Joshua gripped the bed's guardrail. "I wish I knew. Darla was short on details, but I need to do this. How about we change the subject now? Let's talk about your mother's funeral. What are your plans?"

Harold shrugged. "I don't know. I think I may just have them bury her with Dad and then have a memorial service at our house after this is over. I know I can't go through planning something right now—you said so yourself. I won't put Tom through this again, and you're leaving. I'm just not ready to make that decision."

"Okay. I'll let the coroner know and have them hold Barbara's body until you make your final decision. If you do decide to have her buried, I'm sure Maria can handle calling the funeral home to make those arrangements."

"Thanks, Doc. Tom can handle that much as well, so I should be covered."

Joshua stood up. "Well, I need to go and get packed. If something happens and you need me, call."

Both men hugged, and then Harold held on to Joshua's hand.

"Hey, Doc, I do have one question you can answer. What's up with you and Maria? Before Dad's funeral started, you two looked pretty cozy."

A small grin came across Harold's face.

Joshua pulled his hand free. "We can talk about that later too."

"Okay, Doc. I get it. Don't kiss and tell." Harold chuckled.

Despite his best efforts, Joshua blushed. "I'll see you soon, Harry."

"That's right, Doc. Run away. I'm onto you."

CHAPTER 8

THE FLIGHT TO KEY WEST HAD BEEN uneventful. Joshua spent most of his time pondering his own mental health. Was he like Harold? Was he running away from the pain of failure and the loss of his friends? By the time the plane landed, Joshua was convinced he was running toward his problems, not away from them. The answers lay in the blue Caribbean.

The long flight had also allowed him a little time to think about Richard and Barbara. He needed to focus on the good memories. He and Richard enjoyed their sports. Richard would kid him about the Carolina Panthers's losses in the Super Bowl, and Joshua would remind him of the last time a California team played in one. Joshua recalled the employee who put a gun to Richard's head at the office while he was working there for a brief time. Joshua had done his job, calmed the man down, and took away the gun. Richard called him a hero then. Why had Richard not given him the same opportunity to take away his gun?

Joshua grabbed his bags from the claim area and called Darla. She was right outside the terminal. He had to work to keep his jaw shut when he saw her. She looked stunning in her white sundress. The tan accentuated her raven black hair and dark eyes. *If I were a younger man ...* Joshua thought when Darla walked up and shook his hand.

"Hello, Doctor. I hope you had a pleasant flight."

Joshua had to force himself to let go of her hand. "I did."

She smiled. "That's good, because it's time to get on another plane."

Joshua could feel his body sink at the thought. He grabbed his bags and worked to keep up with her. They walked past the terminal and out to a private gate where a Cessna Grand Caravan was waiting. Joshua was winded by the time they reached the plane.

"I guess I'm not the young man I used to be."

Darla patted him on the back as if he were a child. "That's okay, Doctor. I'll be there one day."

"Please, call me Joshua."

He climbed up into the plane, and they took their seats. The prop rumbled to life and Joshua gripped his armrest a little tighter. He felt Darla's hand touch his, and he looked over.

She gave him a compassionate look and spoke over the drone of the engine. "You're not afraid to fly, are you?"

Joshua put on his bravest face. "No. I just don't normally fly in something this small."

Darla tilted her head back, laughed, and returned her attention to him. "It's the only way to get around in the Keys."

Joshua wanted to ask her what was going on, but Darla's grandiose demeanor seemed out of character. He took that as a hint to keep any real questions to himself for the time being. Instead, he sat back and soaked in the view as they left Key West and headed deeper into the Caribbean. The waters were clear enough to see a few sharks and other large fish. A thermal caught the plane, and it shuddered. Joshua looked over at Darla, gave a sarcastic smile, and then turned back to the window. *What am I doing here?* His fingers embedded into the armrest.

The plane flew over a large Key and prepared to land. Joshua noted several bungalows and a large mansion. Carved out of one end of the island was a short airstrip. A small seashell road led from the compound to the airstrip. Well-spaced palm trees lined the roadway and parking areas. Saw grass, mangrove trees, and other shrubs covered most of the island outside of the compound. Whoever owned the Key had made an oasis in the middle of a desert island in the middle of the ocean.

The plane made a smooth landing. Joshua could see Senator Jones, Jerry Guilford, and John Richmond standing in reception as the plane rolled to a stop. The rumble of the prop ceased, and a worker came and opened the door. Darla and Joshua deplaned. John walked up and gave Darla a kiss and a long hug—too long. *Too bad Harold isn't here.* Joshua had to stop his thought as John came up and enthusiastically shook his hand.

"Doctor, I'm so glad you can join us. Welcome to my island. She isn't much, but she's private. I assume Darla has filled you in on the details."

Joshua looked just past John to see a slight shake of Darla's head.

Joshua smiled. "No, I'm afraid we haven't had the time."

"Of course. Well, let's get you settled into your bungalow."

John motioned for the worker to take their bags.

Darla slid her arm around John's waist. "John, why don't you let me fill in Joshua, and then we can all meet."

John leered at Darla, enraptured by her charms.

"That sounds perfect. Why don't you and Joshua take the second Jeep, and we can all get together in a couple of hours at my house by the pool."

He gave Darla a kiss, and the men drove off. The workers already had the empty Jeep packed by the time they walked to the vehicle.

As soon as they sat in the car alone, Joshua looked over at Darla. "What was all that?"

Darla gave him a scowl. "Don't judge my methods, Doctor. Trust me; he won't get beyond a kiss and flirting. These men are extremely dangerous. I suggest you keep any other questions to yourself for now. I think you'll have your answers soon enough. We are here to discuss you joining us since Harold fired you."

Darla cranked up the engine and started down the rough road. Joshua grabbed Darla's hand on the gearshift.

"Fired me? I don't understand."

She shook free of his grip and then returned her hand to the knob. "It's very simple. Harold fired you because you allowed his parents to die. You're upset and want back what he took away. Your home, your online site, all of it." Darla mouthed quietly, "Be careful."

They pulled up in front of a bungalow-style home. "This is where you will be staying while you're with us."

She opened the bolted wooden door and led Joshua in. The bungalow had three rooms with an atrium in its center. Screening kept the larger bugs from finding their way in from the roof to the room where the tree escaped to the sunlight. Solid wooden-framed chairs were neatly paired about the main room. A mahogany door slid into the wall to reveal a beautiful master bedroom with a king-size canopy bed framed by a large oak dresser on one side and a nightstand on the other. The room was kept cool by a wall air conditioner. The two stepped farther into the master suite to the bathroom furnished with a garden-style Jacuzzi, large glass shower, a marble sink, and an elongated toilet sitting at the far end.

Finished with the tour, Darla remained standing in the bathroom and reached into her pocket. She handed Joshua a piece of paper.

Eyes and ears everywhere. We will talk later during our walk.

Joshua nodded, and then to his surprise, she ate the slip of paper. "Wow, I thought that only happened in movies."

Darla smirked as she swallowed.

She led him back to the family room. "As you can see, Joshua, John takes very good care of his guests."

Joshua decided to just roll with her lead. He hoped the answers to his questions were forthcoming.

"Yes, what should I do if I need anything? Phone room service?"

He laughed at his own joke.

"As a matter of fact, yes." Darla pointed to a card on the nightstand next to a phone. "Just pick up the phone. It runs to the servants' quarters. Anything you need—supplies, food, alcohol, you name it."

Joshua walked over and saw the word *Welcome* written in calligraphy on the card. There were no numbers on the telephone, just a single button.

"That looks simple enough."

"Go ahead and unpack, Doctor. I will return for you in an hour."

With that, Darla walked out the door. Joshua walked around the house again. He thought about turning on the television, but knowing they were watching was unnerving. Given the circumstances, he was sure they were monitoring him closely. Joshua hoped for some privacy in the bathroom. If he wanted to relax, that was the place to go.

He gathered some clothes and his shaving kit and went into the bathroom where an empty Jacuzzi awaited. He filled it to the water line near the top and eased in. All the stress and anguish seemed to lift off him. He closed his eyes and let the water console his weary body.

Darla's voice invaded his tranquility. "Joshua!"

He jumped, and a wave of water went rolling over the edge and onto the floor. He began to get his bearings. Darla stood in the doorway.

"Doctor, we need to get moving. We're on a clock. Please hurry up and get dressed."

She turned on her heel and walked out into the main room. Joshua heard the sliding doors close. *I don't know if I'm relieved or upset that it wasn't more awkward.* He supposed it was a little of both. Nobody said getting older was easy. He dried off and dressed in a pair of shorts and a polo shirt. He was still shaking off his grogginess when he and Darla left for the short drive to the main house. It was an impressive home. The Moroccan design, with the red tiled roof and stucco siding, reminded Joshua of California. Walking through the arched entryway, they entered the marble foyer. Polished stone steps led upstairs. He and Darla followed the entryway around to the pool. The house was a blend of outdoor and indoor rooms. The pool was inside the home yet not under a roof. Joshua assumed this was to dissuade any local wildlife.

The three men sat in lounge chairs, drinking.

John sat up and turned to Joshua. "Doctor, care to join us?"

"Thank you. This is my kind of meeting."

Joshua took a free chair next to him.

"Julio, bring the good doctor a rum runner. Doctor, have you had one before?"

Joshua smiled. "I don't believe I have."

"Good. You'll love it."

John sat back again on the chair. Senator Trey Jones spoke up but continued staring at the sky, as if talking to God instead of Joshua.

"Tell me, Doctor, why would a man of healing want revenge on his enemy?"

Joshua chose his words carefully. "I don't seek revenge. I want justice."

Trey smiled. "Well said."

Jerry sat up and looked at Joshua. "Doctor, I assume you have decent savings."

Joshua thought for a moment. *This isn't a meeting; it's an inquisition. Nobody needs to know my business.* The last thing Joshua was going to do was reveal his finances. "I believe that is my business. Let's be honest though, Jerry. Does anyone really have enough money?"

The three men laughed, and Joshua felt his blood go cold.

John sat up and Trey followed his lead. "Good, Doctor. I like your answers. The three of us are of the same mindset. You see, Richard did his best to screw us out of our fair share."

Joshua leaned in. His focus was not a charade. "How so?"

John took a long sip of his drink before answering. "We all started in this business at the same time. Jerry and I wanted to join our companies as one, but Richard would not hear of it. He said we would all come out ahead competing. If we had a monopoly, the government might avoid us and go with a smaller firm just to look like they were getting the best deal for the taxpayer. As if, right, Trey?"

Trey kept considering the heavens.

Joshua spoke up to break the tension. "I take it things didn't work out the way Richard said?"

John stood and paced around his chair. "They worked out all right, for Richard. He managed to undercut us on almost every contract. Jerry and I thought he would at least pad his numbers, so we could all make a little extra cash, but he refused. He said he was making enough and didn't need to pad anything. That's all fine and good when you win all the bids. Isn't that right, Senator?"

Senator Jones didn't budge in his seat. "Yes." It was a flat, bitter response.

"You see, Doctor, we think we know why Richard was so successful. We stumbled upon the answer ourselves. Well, to be honest, my investigators stumbled upon it. You'll meet his reasons a little later."

Senator Jones sat up and glared at John. "Don't you dare go there. Richard was a good man. He knew nothing about my private life. Have some respect for the dead."

John walked over with a smirk on his face and squeezed the senator's shoulder. "Trey, please, don't cause a scene."

Joshua didn't know what was going on, but he felt sorry for the senator. John walked back and sat on his chair.

"Where was I? Oh, yes, we all want what we have coming to us. Senator Jones has been key in helping us remedy that situation. Unfortunately, when Richard committed suicide, it put a kink in our plans. After all, how can we possibly expose the man as a blackmailer if he's dead?"

The senator threw his drink, and it splashed against the window. A worker ran over with a towel to clean up the mess.

"Senator, maybe you should go spend some time with Hye."

Trey stood and left the group.

"You'll have to excuse him. He's under a lot of pressure lately. As I was saying, Richard was blackmailing Trey. I guess he couldn't live with himself if that information came out."

Joshua knew it was a dangerous move, but he had to ask. "It's odd. I never saw anything in Richard that would have led me to think he was a blackmailer or involved in anything illegal."

John came over and sat on Joshua's lounge chair and squeezed his thigh. A shiver ran up Joshua.

"Doctor, I'm not here to judge your abilities as a mental health professional. We're all here for one thing: to get what is rightfully ours."

Joshua thought it was best to play along. "How do I get my share?"

John gave Joshua's knee a slap. "Great question! That's what I like to hear. I need information about Harold."

Joshua stood and stretched his legs. It was as much to remove the stiffness remaining from the trip as it was to get away from John.

"What sort of information?"

John stood up and faced Joshua eye to eye. "Doctor, we know you were there to work with Harold. We all remember he had a horrible temper as a child. Something tells me that never changed, since you were living there and then he threw you out."

Joshua stretched his back and returned to his seat. "You know I can't discuss patient cases, no matter who they are."

John laughed and walked over to Darla, who leaned against the wall, listening. He gave her a long lust-filled look and ran his hand down her back until he finally ran out of flesh he could reach.

"Doctor, I would never dream of demanding you do that. However, if something happened at the house that involved the police or repairmen, well, that's common knowledge. You see, the board would be very interested since he is the front-runner to take over his father's company. Unfortunately, with Harold in place, our bid to take over Parabolic is in jeopardy."

So that was it. The rumors are true. They did try to blackmail Richard with false charges. Joshua knew that John's depraved mind believed he was justified.

"I have an idea, John," Joshua said. "What if I go back? I believe I can get Harold to take me back. He's only angry because of his grief. I'm sure in a few days he'll be calling me. I know how these things run their courses. Once I move back in, I'll keep an eye on Harold. I'm sure something will trigger him. When it does, it's likely to make the news."

John laughed and brought Joshua another drink. "Excellent idea. I'm good at bringing smart people aboard, and Doctor, that is genius. Feel free to enjoy yourself here in my paradise until you hear from him."

"John, do you mind if I give our newest partner a tour of your paradise?" Darla asked

"Excellent idea, my dear. Now, Doctor, be good to my girl. You don't want to get on my bad side."

Joshua shook his head. "No worries. I'm old enough to be her father."

John laughed. "So am I. What's your point?"

Joshua shuddered inside but forced a smile. He and Darla began to walk their way out of the compound. They walked a half mile before reaching the narrow strip of beach.

Darla finally spoke. "We're safe here."

Joshua was thankful she slowed her pace.

"Now do you understand?" Darla asked.

He was still trying to comprehend what he had just been a part of. "I believe so. It's all so surreal. John's a very dangerous man. We should go to the police before things get worse."

"We can't. John pontificating isn't proof."

Joshua stopped. "What do you mean? We both listened to him admit to extortion and more. Why did you bring me out here if it wasn't to be a witness?"

Darla got him walking again. "You are a witness but only to John's speeches. I'm here to get hard proof. If something happens to me, you will need to testify to what I was in the middle of."

She steered them off the sand and into some saw grass and low-growing plants. She pointed to a group of three stones randomly lying near one another.

"Do you see those three rocks?"

Joshua nodded.

"I am keeping copies of everything I find there. If I disappear, send the police here. That's where the proof will be."

Joshua instinctively grabbed her hands like he would a child's. "What if I just stay here?"

"Not a chance. The longer you stay, the more danger we are both in. I want you off the island as soon as you can find a good excuse, and you can't go home. I'm sure John will have you followed. Stay in a hotel for a couple of days. Don't let anyone know you're in town. Then go home like everything is fine again."

He let go of her hands, and they both walked back onto the beach. They continued down the wet sand. A hundred yards farther, they rounded a corner. Senator

Jones was in the arms of a young woman. They heard Joshua and Darla, and both jumped back. The sight before him shocked Joshua. She wasn't a woman at all—she was a girl, no more than fourteen. The senator took her hand, and the two walked away. Darla turned around and Joshua followed suit.

"He's a pedophile? So that's how they're blackmailing him?"

Joshua picked up his pace to avoid losing Darla.

Darla had a hard edge in her voice. "It's worse than you think."

"What could be worse?"

"I don't want to talk about it. You'll know all about that if I make it back."

Joshua gave her a pained look.

"Don't worry about me, Joshua. I'm a big girl. I can handle these boys."

Joshua was not convinced.

Just short of the compound, Darla raised her voice. "That's the island, Doctor. I hope you enjoyed your tour."

Joshua followed suit. "This is a paradise, and I'm famished. What time is dinner on our little island?"

"At five o'clock sharp. Please meet us at John's house. The dining room is next to the pool."

Joshua reached for the door to his bungalow. "I believe I remember. Thank you."

He closed the door behind him and let out a long breath. It took his remaining strength just to make it to the first chair and collapse into its cushions. His eyelids started to close when he looked down at his watch—4:30 p.m. He was too old to be playing spy games.

Joshua forced himself into the shower. Slowly the water began to revive him. He was dressed and out of the door by 4:55 p.m.

The three men sat around a large table. The dining area connected to the vast patio deck via a sliding wall, which was currently retracted. The group had already started on their drinks. Darla stood behind John Richmond's chair and massaged his shoulders. Jerry was the first to notice Joshua. "Doctor, we were taking odds on whether you would come to dinner or take a nap."

"The nap nearly won."

Everyone laughed, and Joshua grabbed a seat between John and Jerry.

"John, I need to return in a couple of days. Harold's doctor tried to contact me yesterday, but I refused the call. I wanted to set the tone so Harold will be begging me to come back. I told Darla during our tour that I don't think it will be hard to walk back in the door."

John smiled and looked around the table. "That didn't take long. I guess he's smaller than he looks."

Joshua tried not to bristle. "Well, to be fair, he watched his parents die."

John laughed. "Big deal! So the kid sees his dad blow his brains out. Do you have any idea what our weapons do to villages or convoys? Sure, they may be the bad guys, but not everyone in a blast zone is guilty. Richard knew; I know. We've all had to witness the results of our weapons' handiwork. Those government boys want to make sure we stay motivated to improve our accuracy. Heck, maybe it was karma for old Richard and Harold.

"Besides, he should be thanking me! He's a rich boy and the biggest winner if his dad's company sells. Harold holds a cool sixty percent of all the stock. Thankfully, the voting shares are equally spread among the board. That whole setup was an idea I gave Richard. I told him that would keep the company from falling under the wrong person's control. How's that for a cruel irony? That means big boy gets all the money from the company and none of the responsibility. Come to think of it, you could argue I had a hand in all of this. Maybe I should ask for a commission from Harold."

Everyone laughed, and Joshua did his best to follow along.

Opposite the pool was a beautiful concrete stepdown deck with a large fountain. Next to it, steps led upstairs to the sundeck and a master suite. Joshua was admiring the architecture when a beautiful Korean woman walked down the steps. Her shiny black hair flowed straight down to the base of her neck. Her hazel eyes pulled Joshua in even though he tried to avoid staring. She was a tiny woman who carried herself with strength and grace. In many ways, she reminded him of Maria. Joshua caught his breath when he saw a teenage girl walk down behind her. The same teenager he had seen on the beach with the senator.

John stood, and all the men followed suit. "Joshua, may I present the senator's companion Hye Nam. This beautiful girl with her is her daughter, Areum. They are the family of the senator's confidant Hoon Nam."

Joshua noticed the barbs the senator shot into John with his eyes.

"Very nice to meet you both."

Joshua stole a quick glance at Darla. The fear in her eyes told him to keep his thoughts to himself. This answered the blackmail mystery. Everyone sat down. He decided it was best not to bring up the newest dinner guest.

Joshua turned to John. "I've been thinking about our business deal. I believe I can be of value to the board. I worked there as a counselor and advisor during Harry's college days. I'll follow up on that as soon as I return. Would email suffice for updates?"

John wrote down an email address and slid it to Joshua.

"Use that address. It's a secure server. On the other side is a web address. Download the program and use it to encrypt your emails."

Joshua took the card and read both sides. "Excellent. Well, gentlemen, as I said before, I am exhausted. If nobody objects, I vote we eat, and then I'm off to bed."

John reached over and shook Joshua's hand. "Welcome aboard. I hope you enjoy tonight's fare. We're serving lionfish and filet." John looked over his shoulder, "Paco, rum runners, water, and food—now, please."

Paco disappeared, and soon a parade of servers and plates appeared. Darla took her seat, and soon everyone was enjoying the feast. They ate in silence. Despite John's megalomania, even he would stop talking long enough to enjoy a gourmet feast. Once he was full, Joshua excused himself. His eyelids and legs felt like lead walking back to his bungalow, and his newly filled stomach only seemed to make his short walk that much more burdensome.

Joshua had not lied; he was exhausted. The sickening display before him only added to the stress of a long day. He lay down on his bed to ponder what he would do, and then his eyelids shut before he could think of a single word.

Joshua awoke the next morning still in his clothes from the night before. He did not feel woozy or have any other side effects he would expect from a drug. He checked his pockets—all his identification was in place. The room itself was exactly as he had left it. He smiled and looked toward the ceiling. *I don't know where the cameras are, but somebody had a very boring night watching an exhausted middle-aged man sleep.*

The clock read seven in the morning. He went to the front window of his bungalow. The island was quiet and still in his view. Not a soul stirred. Joshua showered, changed, and went for a walk. Despite the debauchery, the island had a peace about it when John and his cronies were not running around the place. He followed the familiar trail Darla had traversed with him the day before. He found a large rock to sit down on. The water was glassy and still. Joshua prayed for wisdom.

Stopping these men was no longer an act of personal revenge. Joshua had to protect Harold. Should he simply tell him and allow Harold the joy of beating the men to death? Joshua was surprised by his own brutal instincts. A thought popped into his mind. *This could be the reason behind Richard's silence. These men are far more dangerous than they appear—and worse, they all hold a lot of power. Perhaps Richard was trying to protect me, not block me out.*

The water stirred, and a few feet into the clear teal water, three manatees poked their heads up. They seemed as interested in Joshua as he was in them. The group stared back and forth at one another.

Joshua could not help speaking. "I don't suppose you all have an answer for a bitter old psychiatrist?"

To his surprise, they swam a little closer. Joshua looked up.

"I suppose you will speak through a manatee because the ass obviously doesn't understand."

He smiled and hoped God had a sense of humor. The three sea cows suddenly dropped below the surface. A moment later, a motorboat came roaring around the bend of the beach. John and Jerry sat inside.

John cut the engine and hollered. "Thought you swam away, Doctor! Out for a morning walk?"

"Yes! Just enjoying the peace of your Key!"

Joshua swallowed the annoyance he felt.

"Very good! Breakfast is being served!"

Without another word, John started the boat, turned around, and returned. Joshua had his answer. He had to get back home. John had a close eye on him here. If he stayed in the lion's den, all he would be able to do was watch, and he had seen quite enough.

Breakfast was an almost southern fare with bacon, grits, scrambled eggs, various fruits, and shrimp. The three men left and spent most of their time in John's office together. Joshua attempted to get some time to talk with Darla, but John pulled her into their meeting.

He decided to take advantage of his break and enjoy an afternoon swimming and lying around the pool.

At dinner, the group gathered around the same dining table. This time Hye and Areum did not join them. Joshua remained and enjoyed the cigars and cognac afterward.

"John, I got another call from Harold's doctor. He asked if I would be willing to return and help him."

John looked at Joshua and gave a knowing smile. "They can't handle the brute without you, eh?"

Joshua took a sip of his drink to avoid punching John. He let the warm cognac settle his anger before speaking. "Something like that. As you know, I don't talk about patients."

John started laughing. His cackle sent chills through Joshua.

John calmed himself and said, "Come, Doctor, I was over there for dinner during one of his little 'fits.' The man is a menace. But he could make a powerful ally. What do you think, Trey? Maybe we can get him a job in security after we take over everything."

Everyone laughed. Joshua smiled through his cigar, so his teeth had something to bite down on.

He blew out his smoke in John's direction and put the cigar down. "I'm glad you agree with me, John. I plan to leave as soon as possible tomorrow."

"Very good, Doctor. We've enjoyed your visit."

Joshua smiled. "It has been an experience, thank you. Gentlemen, if you will excuse me, this old doctor needs to get some rest."

The men wished him a good night, and Darla silently nodded. Exhausted and discouraged, he headed inside the bungalow. The men intended to take on Harold. They still wanted everything the family had. What was the point? Were John and Jerry really that bitter over Richard's success? Weaker men had held grudges for less.

Joshua sat on the edge of his bed to think things through. *John mentioned Harry would get most of the money, and he hinted he knew about Harry's condition. He doesn't know Harry's current state. I am sure John was hoping Harry would go berserk at the funeral. He is coldhearted enough to pull such a stunt. I need to move quickly before they decide to take another run at him. At least he's safely locked away in Malibu, and nobody except his doctor, Maria, and I know about it. He could try at Barbara's funeral, but Harry is planning a private memorial, so they could not do it then. This is going to be a race. Who will finish first? Darla and her investigation, or the men and their plans?*

Joshua felt powerless, but he no longer felt like a failure. Anger had replaced the self-pity inside the void of his losses.

Chapter 9

Joshua kept a low profile after waking the next morning. He wanted off the island as soon as possible. Darla flew with him back to Key West and then returned to the island. Joshua took a cab to Duval Street to wait for his red-eye to LAX. Once he was among the crowd, he called Maria.

"Joshua! I have missed you so much."

Joshua instinctively looked around. "How did you know it was me?"

"Your caller ID, silly."

Joshua tried to lean against the building he stood in front of to blend in, but he felt like he still stuck out. "Of course. I need to tell you something. I'm coming home tonight, but I can't be home. It's a long story. Just trust me. I will be home the day after tomorrow. I just wanted you to know I'm safe in Key West."

"I'm so glad. Should I tell Harold?"

"Have you talked to him?"

"He called me once. He is so homesick. We cried about Richard and Barbara. Then he told me how much he loves us. I think Harold is getting better. He sounds more at peace."

Joshua pushed himself off the wall and prepared to end their conversation. "I'm so glad to hear that. I need to go. Oh, and please don't tell Harry. I will explain more when I see you. Until then, my love."

"Oh, Joshua, I can't wait."

He hung up the phone and kept walking. Joshua sat down at a small table located at an outdoor tavern. From there, he would have an unobstructed view of people walking by or standing watching him. The server came up, and he ordered a beer. The brew was smooth and felt good against his parched mouth. Joshua had started to relax when a large man came over and sat down at his table. Joshua looked at him, alarmed.

"May I help you?"

The large man wore a Hawaiian-style shirt, like many middle-aged tourists. Although he could not see his weapon, Joshua was sure he had one.

The man smiled and spoke in a deep but calm voice. "Don't worry, Doctor. John wants to make sure you are safe until you leave tonight."

Joshua took a long swallow of his beer and put down the glass. He wanted to appear calmer than he felt.

"Is there something I should know? This is Key West; my biggest threat is a drunk throwing up on me."

The stranger laughed. "I understand. Consider this an easy duty for both of us."

Joshua signaled the waitress. "Have a beer with me then. This is Key West, after all."

"If you're offering me a beer, you should know who you are drinking with. I'm Jeff."

"Call me Joshua." When the waiter walked up, he said, "Get him whatever he wants."

Jeff smiled. "I'll have what he's having."

Joshua gave the table a light slap. "Well, Jeff, I feel like sightseeing."

Jeff crinkled his forehead slightly. "Did you have someplace in mind?"

Joshua smiled and sipped his beer. He liked Jeff. He could take a break from seeking justice or revenge and just have fun.

"We have to go to the southernmost buoy, of course," Joshua said. "I also would like to see Ernest Hemingway's house and the lighthouse."

Jeff pushed himself into the back of his chair. "You certainly have a list."

Joshua nodded. "I'm a firm believer in taking advantage of every opportunity."

"I like you, Doctor." Jeff chuckled. "You're my kind of man."

Both men enjoyed one another's company. Joshua and he got another tourist to take their photo at the southernmost buoy. They cheesed it up, and Jeff posted it on his Facebook account. At Ernest Hemingway's home, Joshua opined about writing his blog from the Florida Keys one day.

Jeff's response was a warning. "Careful what you wish for."

He said nothing more, and Joshua's gut told him not to drill down further.

Jeff posted more photos of them around Hemingway's house. He even pretended to ghost hunt with the phone's video feature. Joshua noted a pink couch in the home looked very similar to the red one sitting in his living room. He was correct; he had made that room a museum. He would need to change that.

The men moved on to the lighthouse. Joshua loved the view of the surrounding homes and ocean from atop the lighthouse. The white-roofed bungalows amidst the thick green trees across the flat Key were very different from his Malibu view. Jeff took several pictures and sent them to Joshua in an email. By the time they had finished walking the grounds, it was time for Jeff to take Joshua to the airport.

The men got into Jeff's car. Jeff dialed a number on his phone and put it on speaker. John's voice answered.

"Doctor, I trust you had an enjoyable day at Key West. Jeff was sending me photos. I want to make sure you are still having an enjoyable time. We are watching your trip, so you don't have to worry about anything."

Joshua could not hide the shock on his face. "John, I appreciate everything you've done. Really, we aren't in some dangerous part of the world. I am fine traveling alone. I will add that Jeff is a great tour guide."

Joshua could hear John's cackle through Jeff's phone.

"Doctor, there are dangers everywhere. That's one of the first things you learn in my business. Jeff, you did an excellent job today. Come on back home after the doctor's plane leaves."

"Yes, sir." Jeff said nothing more before hanging up on John. He started the car and then looked over at Joshua. "Sorry, man. I can see you feel spied on, and I guess you were. I like you, Joshua. Take some advice—don't get too close to John. He's a dangerous dude."

Joshua could see the pained look on Jeff's face. He was being sincere. Joshua focused and used the same smooth voice he would with Harold when he was counseling him.

"Don't worry, Jeff. I don't plan on getting close to John. We have some business together. Once we complete that, we are parting ways. He is not the type of guy I hang around with."

Jeff put the car in gear and started down the road. "Good."

The rest of the ride to the airport was silent.

On the flight home, Joshua tried to focus on his day with Jeff rather than the horrors he had experienced on the island. He would stay near LAX for the night and then decide if he would really return home or wait a few more days. Joshua missed Maria desperately, but John seemed to have eyes everywhere, and he needed to protect her, as well.

Once he arrived in Los Angeles, he checked into the Embassy Suites, picked up the phone, and called Maria before he fell asleep in his clothes again.

"Joshua, are you back?"

Joshua rose off the bed and began to walk around his room. "I'm no longer in Florida."

"Oh, good. I will see you tomorrow?"

Joshua could hear the excitement and anticipation in her voice.

He gazed out his top floor window. "I'm afraid not, honey. It's just not safe. I'm not Darla. I don't know how to tell whether I am being followed. John had me escorted when I was in Key West. I never saw the guy coming, and I was looking. He just sat down at my table, introduced himself, and we started talking. It's too dangerous to come home yet."

Maria's voice raised in fear. "Joshua, I'm scared for you! What will you do?"

He sat down at the desk and bowed his head while he spoke. His shoulders tightened and began to ache. "I'm okay. Just trust me, Maria. Call Harold and tell him I will pick him up from the hospital when he is released. I will see you in a few days."

He could hear Maria begin to sniffle into the phone. "I trust you, Joshua. I will see you soon."

"Until then, love."

"I love you, Joshua."

He hung up the phone and prepared to get some rest.

The remaining week and a half would be the break that Joshua needed. He and Dr. Gutierrez had spoken only a couple of times. Harold had embraced his mandate to rest. Although he shared a couple more dreams with Dr. Gutierrez, none had resulted in the violent fits he had experienced in the hospital.

Joshua had spent his days making generous use of the hotel's pool, Jacuzzi, and gym. He played the tourist and took the shuttle to the nearby beach. In the evening, he would enjoy his free cocktails. He met a fellow North Carolinian who was there for an engineering conference on earthquake structures. The two discussed football and argued whether the University of North Carolina was a better school than North Carolina State University.

The time passed more quickly than Joshua thought it would. He found himself smiling on the shuttle ride back to LAX to pick up his car. The smile slowly faded as he got closer to Malibu. He had seen the devil, and now he would have to face him. He was not alone, but Joshua felt a great burden to protect Harold and Maria rather than have them join the fight. He pulled into the parking lot at Avalon Malibu. It was time to begin the battle of his life.

Chapter 10

MARIA WAS WAITING FOR THE MEN as they drove up to the front entrance of the estate. Joshua had called ahead to make sure the house was ready. He felt a bit embarrassed when Maria hugged him in front of Harold. The men had not seriously discussed Maria in their brief time together in the car. Given the sideways smile he gave Joshua, Harold appeared to already know about them. Maria took in the bags, and Harold invited Joshua for a swim in the infinity pool. He wanted to talk and watch the sunset. Joshua had never seen this side of Harold. *His time at Avalon seems to have done some good.*

Joshua headed up to his house, got his trunks, and joined Harold at the pool. The water was crisp, and Joshua dove under its refreshing surface. He found Harold leaning on his arms at the edge of the pool. He was staring out over the Pacific and ignoring everything else around him. Joshua swam over and joined Harold at its edge.

Harold did not move as he spoke. "You know, Doc, it's these moments when I can forget how bad everything is. There are people out there who will have children shot, parents beat up, you name it. All they have when they come home is more despair. I come home to this. If there is a God, he knows my breaking points and when to pull me back."

Joshua leaned against the pool to take in the glowing sunset. "You have been through a lot in just a few weeks. I have to confess, you're looking happier than I thought you would."

"Well, Doc, I can't explain it. There was no single moment when I can say I suddenly feel happy again. In fact, I had more visions when I was at Avalon. I had the usual visions of killing John, Jerry, and Trey. The same things I saw when you hypnotized me in your office. Honestly, that part of my vision didn't even faze me. It was Bill. Bill would show up in my dreams. I don't know why he was there, but it reminded me I have more family out there somewhere. Even if we don't know each other."

Joshua turned around and put his elbows on the edge of the pool. He was silent for a moment. "Do you remember your brother?"

Harold stood and turned toward Joshua. "Not really. I mean, I have an impression of him. A vague memory of a baby. I remember crying when Richard and Barbara took me and they left Bill at the orphanage. I didn't understand at the time why Bill had to stay at the orphanage for our birth mother. But I also remember how happy I was to have ice cream later that day. I guess it wasn't that big of an impact on me."

"How did you know the man in your vision was Bill?"

Harold splashed some water on his shoulders and returned to watching the sun sink on the ocean's horizon.

"He told us. That's what we were talking about when John and his stooges appeared."

Joshua turned back around. His forehead wrinkled in thought, and he all but lost sight of the glory in the sky before him. "What did Bill look like?"

Harold smiled as he spoke. "He was sort of like you, Doc. An inch taller, maybe. He had hair like mine, except it was black. We look a lot alike. He's just a little shorter."

Joshua could think of only one word. "Interesting."

Harold turned and faced Joshua. "Why, Doc? Do you know what my brother looks like?"

Joshua turned to Harold. "I know what he used to look like. I had a picture of him when he was eighteen. I'm not sure if I even still have it. After we get through your mother's funeral and we take care of the people who caused your parents' deaths, we can talk more about your brother."

"That sounds good, Doc."

"Speaking of the funeral, do you need me to make the plans?"

Harold shook his head. "No. Just look around us. It's so peaceful here. I've decided to have Mom buried next to Dad without a funeral. We'll do a memorial service here at the house later."

"Later when?"

Harold stood up to his full height and gripped the edge of the pool. "After we get these guys. They've taken away so much. I may feel happier, Doc, but I still want them to face justice."

Joshua grinned. Harold was still on board. He decided to let Harold in on a little of what he had found.

"I'm glad you feel that way. You should know, they have stolen a lot more than government contracts. I wish I could tell you everything I have been through while you were gone. We need to wait for Darla, though. If I had my way, these men would simply disappear from the earth."

Harold jumped back in the water and mocked feeling shocked. "Doc! I thought psychiatrists were all about forgiveness."

Joshua's face darkened, and his voice became cold. "Sometimes it's easier to forgive after people are brought to justice. This is deeply personal, Harry. These men managed to completely shake my confidence and all but destroy my life's work. I haven't been the same. Every day I wonder what mistakes I have made. What advice have I put on that blog that destroyed somebody's life?"

Harold splash a little water at Joshua. "Doc, why would you do this to yourself? What if Dad had come to you? Then what?"

Joshua was in no mood to play around. This matter was too serious. "Based on what I know? I would have told him to sell the company, and we would start something else. Expand what we had done with my business. Perhaps start a whole new defense company or move into aircraft. There were options—or at least, there appeared to be. I think if he had just gotten out of John and Jerry's way, he might have been left alone."

Harold shook his head. "I don't know, Doc. Dad was a smart man. I think he would have thought of all those things. We don't know enough. Until we do, I think you shouldn't beat yourself up."

Joshua turned around and stared out toward the darkening ocean. "You aren't the psychiatrist whose closest friend shot himself."

Harold's voice got soft and low. "No, I'm his son, and I was in the room."

Both men stared out at the final remnants of the bright burning ball that settled into the ocean in the distance. Joshua felt selfish, but Harold could not understand the hell he had been through himself.

With the sun settled below the horizon, the deck and pool lights came on. The men got out of the pool. Joshua's self-pity had waned, but he was too embarrassed by his comments to say anything to Harold. They toweled off. Harold gave Joshua a gentle pat on the back.

"I love you, Doc. Let's just remember who the bad guys are."

Joshua's head dropped down. "Sorry, Harry."

Harold lumbered up the stairs to the back door. Joshua sat there for a moment. Why had his life become all about himself? He had never put his own concerns above someone else.

The back door opened above. Maria came walking out and sat down close next to him.

"Are you okay? Harold said he was worried about you."

Joshua held her hands in his. "I don't know what's going on with me. I just tried to tell Harold my life was falling apart because I'm the psychiatrist whose closest friend shot himself."

Maria squeezed his hand. "Joshua! That isn't you. You're not that thoughtless."

"I know. I know."

Joshua slumped and lowered his head.

Maria let go of his hand and raised his chin, so he was facing her. "This guilt is making your soul dark. You know you should forgive them."

Maria gently rubbed his back with her hand.

Joshua smiled. "You're the second person to say that to me today."

"Who else told you?"

"Harry."

"Then why won't you?"

Joshua slowly shook his head. "I'm not sure I know how. I used to know. I should know—I'm a psychiatrist. That's a big part of the job description. 'Teach people how to forgive and let go of bitterness.' I claim to pray to a God that forgives. I guess this is making me a hypocrite too. If you saw what I saw, Maria, I'm not sure you could forgive them, but that shouldn't matter. Forgiveness is up to me, not them. I have the answers, but I can't seem to accept them."

She wrapped her arms around Joshua and rested her head on his shoulder. "You know Harold and I love you."

Joshua nodded. "I know."

"No, Joshua. I love you. You know, like a woman loves a man she wants to live her life with."

The revelation slammed into his bitterness so hard he felt his chest tighten. Then the warm joy of the truth filled his body. *This beautiful woman ten years my junior loves me. When I am at my worst, she loves me.*

When bitterness is creeping around my soul, she still loves me. Do I want to spend my life with her?

"I love you, too, Maria, but even that worries me."

Maria stopped rubbing his back. "Worries you?"

"What if my love is due to your kindness and my desperation to escape this darkness? I don't want to hurt either of us. I can't stop loving you, but I don't want to rush into anything more serious until we can get all of this resolved. Then we can see if our love can last a lifetime."

Maria kissed him on the cheek and tightened her grip. "You are still the man I love. I can wait. I waited this long. You know I am a very patient woman. Just don't give up."

He smiled. "I promise I won't."

Chapter 11

Joshua and Harold spent their days slowly combing through Richard's documents. He wanted to make sure there was nothing they had missed on Richard's laptop. They were no closer to finding any legal proof, and their frustration levels were rising. Joshua had seen and heard that a conspiracy against Richard existed. Darla might be getting the proof she needed, but he had to do his part. Harold recommended patience and to wait until Darla resurfaced, but Joshua could not stop his obsession

Maria would come over to Joshua's house at night and bring him wine and cheese. He looked forward to her visits. She reminded him there was still beauty and hope in the world. They would sit on the front porch looking over the hills, Malibu, and the Pacific while enjoying each other's company. Joshua would explain to Maria some of the cultural aspects of North Carolina. They discussed NASCAR, BBQ, and bluegrass. Maria would tell him some of the stories her parents told her of Mexico's greatness before the cartels arrived.

Harold and Joshua got together for the morning coffee and daily strategy meeting at the kitchen table.

"I'm at a dead end, Doc. There is nothing on either computer. We have looked at everything. The only thing I've learned is that the company is in a lot of trouble, and I have my work cut out for me."

Joshua took a sip of his coffee. "I haven't found anything either. The only thing I know is that these men are very smart. The emails they sent your dad did not reveal anything. Have you tried your dad's office at Parabolic?"

Harold stretched his arms over his head, and the back of the chair groaned under its burden. "I did. Nothing there. To be honest, I could look closer, but I'm busy. I need to learn the business areas of Parabolic Defense Systems I don't already know."

Joshua put down his cup. "Why don't you look closer? I thought the board had things under control. Isn't the COO running things?"

Harold took a long breath and slowly released it. "Easy, Doc. They do, but if I hope to take over like Dad wanted, I have to show I'm ready."

Joshua took a sip of coffee and scowled. "Don't you own your parents' shares in the company?"

"I do. Around sixty percent of all the stock."

"I thought the company is private anyway. If you have sixty percent of the company, you make the decisions."

Harold shook his head. "It's not that simple, Doc. First, the board has been with Dad since the beginning. It's their thirty percent that helped build the company. Secondly, there are voting shares, and those are evenly distributed so no one person can run the company now."

Joshua's fist came down on the kitchen table in frustration. "But they've been benefitting. I'm not seeing why there is any drama here. You went to Columbia Business School. CEOs are high-level thinkers. You just need management skills and an acumen for business. You should be able to handle that."

Harold put his hand on top of Joshua's, and Joshua's rising anger began to calm a little. "Doc, you worked there in HR while I was in college."

Joshua's mind and emotions cooled down with the triggered memory. "Yes, I was a counselor. There wasn't anything special going on there. Except the occasional worker who had concerns about building missiles. They normally experienced a crisis of conscience after some military or terrorist strike. I helped them learn to deal with it. I didn't see anything going on that someone like you couldn't handle."

Harold released his hand and took a sip of coffee while he stared at Joshua. He put down the cup and moved his face closer. "Unfortunately, it isn't up to you. There are a few hoops I must jump through. First, they are doing a security clearance review. Next, I will meet with the board for the job interview. They will check my knowledge of the company's history, our current weapons projects, and my father's vision for the company."

Joshua paused. Harold had to pass an interview? He had assumed Harold's future was set, like John had said. Why was he listening to John about anything?

"What if you don't pass?"

"Dad wanted to make sure his company was in good hands. If I couldn't, or wouldn't, step up to the plate, the board has the option to bring in who they want. It must be unanimous either way. That's to keep anyone from gaining a political majority."

"Oh, that does make it tougher."

Both men sat back and quietly sipped on their coffee while Harold's challenges sank in.

Harold put down his mug and smiled. "Yeah, I'll pass their tests. I know the answers. If for some reason they reject me, though, I can appeal, and the employees hold an election. If I get a majority, I get the job."

Joshua pretended to sip the coffee that touched his lips. He had no idea Richard's transition of power was so onerous. He lowered his mug.

"That seems highly unusual."

"Dad never forgot his time as a machinist and mechanical engineer. He also knew his board. These are powerful men who like to have things their way. If they did decide to create a coup and attempt to take over the company, Dad wanted to make sure I could hang on to it."

Joshua began to realize how little he knew about the actual business world. His voice was contrite in his reply. "Your dad was a wise man."

The cell phone in his pocket interrupted their conversation.

The caller ID showed *Unknown*. He answered anyway. "Dr. Zeev."

The familiar voice of a woman spoke on the other end. "This is Darla. I wanted to check in and see how Harold is."

Joshua looked over at Harold and smiled. "He is back home. Thank you for asking."

"Is he accepting visitors?"

"One moment." Joshua lowered the phone without hitting the mute button. "Harry, it's our friend. She's back on the coast. Do you have time for her to drop by for a visit?"

A large smile came across Harold's face. "Yes."

Joshua smiled and put the phone back to his ear. "Anytime that works for you."

"You'll be hearing from me."

Darla hung up.

Harold put both his large hands on the table and leaned forward like a child looking at a candy display. "What time is she coming by?"

Joshua loved to see Harold happy, but he knew the news she carried was anything but good. A scowl replaced his smile, and his voice became solemn. "I didn't have a chance yet to update you on everything. She called yesterday before you woke up. All she would say is that she has valuable information, but she couldn't share it on the phone. I don't know what Darla found, but she sounds troubled."

Harold's eyes widened, and his fingers tapped the table. "So, what time is she coming today?"

Joshua sighed. Harold was obviously obsessed with other thoughts when it came to Darla. He decided to reemphasize Darla's situation.

"She wouldn't tell me. I'm guessing she's concerned about her security."

Harold's hands formed into two large fists. "Should we be worried?"

Joshua had gotten through to him, but then a thought popped back in his head. *What are you doing? You can't push Harry like this. Look at his fists. You want him concerned but not angry. It isn't just the furniture you need to be concerned with. He could go and blow the whole operation running after John if he thinks he's threatening Darla.*

Joshua attempted to lighten the mood he had created. "Come on, Harry. Darla is a big girl. You saw how she took you on when she was here. Besides, I didn't think these men worried you."

Harold relaxed his hands, leaned back in his chair, and tapped the table with his fingertips. "I'm not worried, but it's like you said, Darla isn't afraid of me. If she is afraid to speak where others can hear, that says there is a big problem."

Joshua's forehead wrinkled as he leaned back. "Good point, but Darla is a careful woman and good at her job. I'm sure these precautions are just that."

Harold finished the last drops in his mug. "I hope you are as good a tactician as you are a psychiatrist."

Harold meant his words as a compliment and a jest. Joshua's mind took them as a guilty reminder of his recent failure.

"I hope I'm better," he responded quietly.

Harold shook his head at Joshua's last statement, and Maria walked in from her cleaning to interrupt the conversation. Joshua noticed her tight-fitting pants and t-shirt. It was her normal attire for cleaning the house, but here and now her appearance was a ray of light pulling him from a dark cave. She leaned up against the kitchen island, looking spent from her morning chores.

Her voice sounded like a chorus of angels in Joshua's head.

"Mr. Harold, if it is okay, I would like to go grocery shopping."

Harold turned to face her. "Of course. Maria, my parents trusted you to keep our estate in order. I won't be any different. Feel free to do whatever you think is best. I'm always around for questions if you need me."

"Wait!" Joshua yelled and jumped to his feet.

Maria startled and stood up straight. Harold looked around, expecting to find a stranger somewhere in the room.

Joshua stood there, prepared to physically stop Maria. "Harry, don't you think we should have her stay until Darla arrives? We don't know what news she has. Just to be on the safe side."

Harold's lips puckered and then he asked, "Why, Doc? What's changed from this morning?"

Joshua calmed himself and sat back down in his chair. He looked over at Maria's confused and frightened stare. He looked back at Harold. Harold's slightly scrunched up forehead and tweaked eyebrows told him he had overreacted. Why was he suddenly fearful for Maria's safety? The answer returned to his mind, but this time Joshua spoke in a more thoughtful tone.

"Darla coming back is what's different. Yesterday we assumed they were all on the other side of the country on John's 'Pleasure Island.' Today we don't know where anyone is."

Harold nodded his head and gave a reassuring smile to Maria. "Of course, how silly of me."

Maria's body relaxed, and she walked over and stood behind Joshua's chair. Her hands moved to his shoulders, and she started to rub them. Joshua's body melted under her touch. Her soothing voice brought a smile to his face.

"Miss Darla is coming to visit?"

Harold gave Joshua a look that seemed to say he had given too much away. He knew Harold was right. Besides, protecting Maria was not just about keeping her away from harm. He had to make her feel safe.

His tone was warm, and this time Joshua responded with a request instead of a demand. "Yes, would you mind waiting?"

Maria's right hand gently patted Joshua's right shoulder. "My pleasure."

Harold's large body rose and towered over them both, but his words were those of a brother. "Doc, why don't we stop for now? I'm sure you and Maria would like some time together, and I need to get back to studying for my interviews."

Chapter 12

A FEW HOURS LATER, Maria was in the kitchen preparing lunch when Joshua heard the doorbell sound. He stepped out of his office to see who it was. He could hear Maria and Darla's voices and left to greet Darla. Joshua walked into the foyer to find the warm sunlight streaming through the door and Harold greeting Darla.

Harold stuck out his hand. "I'm so glad you returned. Would you like to join us for lunch?"

Darla's voice was soft and smooth, and she looked Harold directly in the eye. "I'd love to."

Harold had yet to release Darla's hand, or her eyes, when he spoke to Maria. "Maria, let's have lunch on the deck."

"I will bring it shortly."

Maria glanced over at Joshua with a short smile and walked out of the entryway.

Harold finally released her hand. He and Joshua escorted Darla to the sundeck and sat down at a table. Joshua noticed Harold could not take his eyes off her. His eyes twinkled with a spark of life Joshua had not seen in Harold for a long time. Darla was beautiful, as usual. She had done something to her hair, but Joshua wasn't sure what it was. Perhaps it was the ponytail.

The outfit formed around her curves, also as usual. She situated her legs where Harold would notice them, and he did.

Harold smiled and unexpectedly took her hand again for a moment. "I'm so glad you made it back safely. I trust everything went okay?"

He released her hand, but she let it linger for a moment before she pulled it back.

"Yes. Although I will say this is one of the more dangerous assignments I have done in a while."

Harold's look changed. Concern tightened his features, and a touch of anger darkened his tone. "Dangerous how?"

"As Joshua knows, John has a secluded island. I had to find places to hide evidence. That's not easy when you have mangroves, palm trees, sand, and coral. Thankfully, John leaves a part of the island undisturbed on one end. The downside was the saltwater crocodiles. I just had to be extra careful getting to it in the dark."

Harold smiled. "You are a woman of many hidden talents." But then his tone changed. "Wait, did you say Joshua was on the island?"

Harold looked over at Joshua. It was obvious he was not going to let this go.

Joshua looked at Darla. She appeared to have every intention of staying out of this part of the conversation. Joshua cleared his throat.

"Harry, when you were in the hospital, I flew out to the island."

Harold's voice rose. "You what?"

Joshua knew he needed to tread lightly. "Harry, you told me I could go if it was important to me."

Harold let his large hands slap loudly on the table, and both Darla and Joshua jumped. "I didn't think you were serious! What if I had needed you? Honestly, Doc. This obsession of yours is taking over your judgment. I'm sure Darla had things under control. What did you add by going to this island?"

Joshua looked confused. "How can any of this be news to you? I sat there in your hospital room and told you I was leaving."

Harold's question mixed with anger and fear. "Then why don't I remember it?"

Joshua sat quietly for a moment. "Perhaps it was the drugs. I didn't ask Dr. Gutierrez what medications he was giving you that morning. I was just concerned with you waking up."

Joshua felt relieved to hear Darla's voice immediately behind his own. "Harold, I called Dr. Zeev and requested his presence. Like I said, it was dangerous. I was concerned I wouldn't get out with my life. I wanted to make sure somebody knew what was going on and where to find the evidence I was hiding."

Harold turned to Darla. The gleam in his eye had dimmed. "What is this, another conspiracy? Doc is no spy. If it were that dangerous, why not simply email the information?"

Darla adjusted her posture, pulling her legs back to a more business appropriate stance. "Harold, if you will let me tell you what I found, I think you will understand why I did what I did. Everything on the island was monitored. Communication by emails, even phone calls, was very dangerous."

Joshua now spoke up in Darla's defense. "It's true, Harry. They followed and monitored me the two days I was there. They even had me followed in Key West while I waited for my flight home."

Darla looked over at Joshua, slightly surprised. He had not had a chance to tell her about his trip home. A silence hung while everyone tried to think of what to say next.

Harold took a long deep breath and finally asked his next question. "Well, tell me what happened then. Who was there?"

"John, of course. Also Senator Jones and Jerry."

Harold looked almost annoyed by her obvious answer. "Was anyone else there?"

Darla attempted to shift her body language back into a friendlier pose, obviously trying to quell Harold's rising tension. "Yes, and this is where things get creepy and start to make a little more sense. You may have seen the senator on television with an advisor named Hoon Nam. He's originally from South Korea."

Images of Trey and Hoon's daughter on the beach rushed back into Joshua's memory. He began to feel queasy thinking about what they saw on the beach when he was there.

Harold leaned in toward Darla and responded in a flat voice. "Yes, I know him. My parents had him over for dinner parties with the senator."

Darla gave Joshua a quick glance. "He has a very beautiful wife and daughter, Hye and Areum."

Harold noticed Joshua's pallor. "Doc, I take it from your pale complexion you know something about this?"

Joshua's voice was a mix of anguish and anger. "Yes, let Darla explain. I can't stomach the memories."

Harold pushed himself against the back of his chair, and it groaned under the strain. "I met Hye when they were here a couple of times, but I haven't met their daughter."

He bent down toward Darla and rested his elbows on his knees, fully sucked into the tale of horror.

Darla's lip curled into a faint snarl. "That's probably because his daughter was too young for dinner parties. In fact, Areum is only fourteen now. She and her mother accompanied the senator to the island."

"I think I know, but where was Hoon?"

Harold's voice was a whisper. Joshua could tell that Harold knew his answers before he asked Darla.

Darla continued, "I don't know, but he wasn't there. Hye and Areum stayed in the main house as John's guest, along with the senator. John and Jerry stayed in bungalows. I assume I don't need to spell out that Hye stayed in the senator's bedroom with him."

"What?" Harold's head drooped down.

Darla grabbed Harold's hands, and he looked back up into Darla's eyes. "Stay with me, Harold. It will make sense soon. During the day, the CEOs and Senator Jones would spend their time at the main house. Normally by the pool. I managed to stay close enough to listen to them talk about business when they were there. They would spend some of the days on John's fishing boat, but the evenings always belonged to the senator and Hye."

Maria walked out. "Excuse me, would you like something to drink while I finish making lunch? It should be ready in five minutes."

Harold sat up and blinked as if he were coming out of a dream. His voice was husky in its reply. "I think we can all use a beer, but please hold off on lunch until Joshua comes in and asks for it. I'm afraid we've gotten involved in our meeting and need to get this out of the way first."

Maria nodded her head. "Yes, sir."

She turned on her heels and strolled back into the house.

Harold turned back to Darla. "Please wait for just a moment. She will be right back."

Joshua decided to change the subject while they waited. "Darla, are you in any danger? You sounded worried when I spoke with you earlier."

Darla looked over at Joshua with a smile. "I'm fine. I just wanted to make sure nobody had followed me. I didn't want this getting linked back to either of you."

Joshua looked past the beauty of her eyes and read her face. He needed to be sure everything was okay, for everybody's sake. "So you will be okay after you leave here today?"

Darla smirked. "Like I said, I can handle myself."

Maria emerged with large glasses of beer and placed them on the table.

Joshua caught her eye. "Thank you. I'll be in after a while."

Maria smiled, replying as she walked inside, "I will be waiting."

Harold cleared his throat and shot Joshua a quick glance. "Please continue, Darla."

Darla once again held Harold's attention with her legs and soft voice as she continued her tale. "I had to work to get John's trust."

Harold stopped breathing. Joshua saw his face turn red and then pale.

"How did you gain his trust?"

The question was a plea.

Darla stared into Harold's eyes and gave a knowing smile. "Not like you are thinking, Harold. Really, you men all think alike. Yes, I flirted, but that was all. Ask the doctor."

Harold looked at Joshua. *Thanks for putting me on the spot, Darla. Should I tell him what I thought I saw?* Joshua knew better than to give his own opinion.

"It's true, Harry. She just flirted."

Darla smiled at Joshua and winked, and then returned her gaze to Harold. "As I was saying, I had to gain his trust. Believe me, there were times I was afraid he might insist on more, but John is a smart guy. He loves money more than women, and he wanted me for my intelligence on Richard's work. He also intended on me working for their little trio to gather dirt on any of their enemies. Fortunately, playing the jilted girlfriend of the late Richard Brown gained me favor not only for my body but for what I represented. I was a pawn that John could use over Harold. He assumed he could blackmail Harold to keep his dad's reputation intact, given Richard's death and the company's current financial position. Over time, they relaxed their surveillance on me, and I had my run of the place. Which brings me to the businesses I discovered."

Darla reached into her shoulder bag and pulled out several papers. Joshua and Harold leaned over the table and read them over as Darla walked them through what she had found.

"These three are partners in two shell companies. One is in Germany. From there, they have a subsidiary that is in the Caymans. That company, called Island Dreaming, owns a full third of the stock in both defense companies. The three of them made hundreds of millions of dollars when Senator Jones introduced the bill to change the weapons strategy away from Parabolic Defense Systems. I have copies of an email the senator sent to his committee. He outlines how the contract changes would cause Parabolic to lay off over half its force. That would increase the supply of skilled labor in the area, allowing both JRA and GDS to pick up the added headcount they would need at a cheaper rate, effectively giving the workers of Parabolic a fifteen percent pay cut to go back to work in the area. Cheaper labor means cheaper contracts, and the government likes that, no matter what the fallout is. There was another email exchange between the senator, Guilford, and Richmond discussing how cheaply they could buy out Richard after he ran out of money."

"What is the other shell company for?"

"I am guessing they use it to sell their weapons to countries the United States prohibits but Europe does not."

Harold took a long sip from his beer. Joshua followed suit but more to settle his imprinted memories of the trip than the news he had heard thus far. Harold put down his glass.

"How does Guilford work into all of this?"

Darla rearranged her papers. "They were childhood friends. Jerry also has more cash than John. John used their friendship to gain access to Jerry's liquidity to set up the shell companies. Jerry appears to be more of a silent partner. I think John keeps him in the loop to ensure he is an accomplice, as well as a bankroll."

Joshua was frustrated. This did not explain why Richard would shoot himself. His voice rose as he presented his question to Darla and Harold. "The senator made a lot of money. Why would Richard shoot himself over that? John Richmond had something else in mind. You remember, Darla. At the island, he was obsessed with taking over the company and destroying Richard's legacy. He was planning something more than a buyout of Parabolic and simply cutting the workforce. Richmond seemed fixated on taking over everything and everyone around his sphere of influence."

Darla turned toward Joshua. "Very perceptive, Doctor. John had a very big tool in his toolbox that he intended to use on every target he could find. You see, the good Senator Jones didn't have a problem sleeping with Hye in front of the other men because they knew. Not only did they know but they were blackmailing the senator. I had a lot of time when they were fishing, and security started to ignore me. I found old emails on John's computer where he threatened to go to Hoon about the affair. I'm sure the senator's wife would not have approved, to put it mildly."

Harold slapped his large hand on the table. "So, we have them! We can expose this whole thing. I assume you have copies?"

"Of course. I printed them out, and you have an encrypted email I sent from my car before I rang your doorbell." She pulled out a stack of papers. "The password is on the top."

Harold smiled. "You are both beautiful and efficient."

"Wait, no, that isn't right," Joshua said.

Harold looked shocked. "Excuse me, Doc?"

Joshua grabbed the edge of the table and shook his head. "No, not about Darla. About this whole thing. This has nothing to do with Richard's suicide. Did you find out anything else? What about Areum and what we saw? Does that work into any of this?"

Darla smiled, and Joshua noticed Harold smiling with her without even knowing why.

"Harold, you should keep him around," Darla said. "He pays much closer attention."

Harold blushed at the faux rebuke.

"Doctor, there is more. It's probably the most important, and sickest, piece of the puzzle. It seems the righteous senator likes little girls."

"What?"

Harold stood up and began to pace. Joshua joined him, not for the news they would hear, but from the stress of already knowing. *That kiss I saw on the beach was enough. What other perversions must we endure in our nightmare?*

"Are you sure both of you are ready to hear this?"

Darla took a long swallow of her beer. The men both took their seats and finished off half a glass in one swallow.

"Doctor, there is more to this than what we saw. Are you sure you want to stay for this part?"

Joshua slowly nodded his head and then let it hang down. "Yes, I need to know all of it."

Harold's surprised voice cut into Joshua. "Doc! You knew?"

Darla came to Joshua's rescue. "Harold, please. Dr. Zeev only knows part of the horror. When he was there, I took him and showed him where I was hiding evidence. We walked further down the beach and came upon the senator and the fourteen-year-old girl kissing. It's something neither of us wants to remember. I'm sure the doctor never wants to repeat his story, even to you."

Joshua looked at Harold. Harold must have seen the pain on his face. His eyes welled up with compassion and love, much like the time Joshua hurt himself playing baseball with Richard and Harold.

"Doc, I'm sorry. You went through that to help me?"

Joshua had to confess. "Not just for you, Harry. For both of us."

The three sat in silence for a couple of minutes. Joshua's memories of the trip haunted his mind.

Darla broke the silence. "I need to continue."

Harold appeared to come out of whatever daze he found himself lost in. "I'm sorry, Darla. Please keep going."

She took a deep breath. "Hye would take a nap every afternoon from one to three. I don't know if he kept her up half the night or if it was just her routine. Either way, it was like clockwork. Senator Jones and Areum would go over to the pool house during that time and do things I can never unsee. Worst of all, Mr. Guilford and Richmond were often at the pool when they would wander into their little love cottage."

Joshua could not hold in his shock. "Why would they allow that?"

"I wondered the same thing. It sickened me. Then I came across an email. Somehow these two CEOs had found out about it. I'm assuming John Richmond had someone like me following the senator. It seems to be John's style. When he wants to take something from someone, he tries to dig up dirt on them and use that as leverage. Like most blackmail, it never stops with the first request. John and Jerry threatened to expose the affair with Areum. This would not only destroy Senator Jones's career but ruin his reputation and likely send him to jail. I don't think a politician and child molester would do very well in prison. Evidently, Trey knew this too.

"John demanded he start an investigation into Richard for bribery and false bids to get all the defense contracts away from Parabolic. Even the hint of corruption could ruin the company's security clearance and destroy it. John claimed to have photos showing Richard with other women. I found a photoshopped image on John's computer. They had removed the senator from a photo with Areum and pasted in Richard."

Harold slammed his fist on the table, and glasses nearly fell over from the reverberation. "My dad would never do such a thing! All their so-called evidence has to be fake."

Darla reached over and laid her hand on top of Harold's. Her voice was calm and soothing as she continued. "That's true. However, in politics, the truth oftentimes does not matter. Budget overruns happen. Dinners or a night on the town can be twisted into something more sinister. They would have ruined your father. Worse, it would have ruined your family's reputation. It would have cost millions in legal fees to stay out of prison and settle lawsuits. Although the photo was fake, can you imagine what that would have done to your mother and you? Your father shot himself to stop them from doing this."

Joshua sat confused. "How did Richard know? We never found proof of this."

Darla released Harold's hand. "It was a phone call the night before his suicide. John sent an email to Jerry telling him he had called Richard on his cell phone. I had the office phone bugged but not your dad's cell. That's why none of us knew what transpired. John warned Richard about the investigation. He tried to use it as leverage to blackmail Richard to sell the company. Obviously, Richard knew better than to trust John at that point."

Harold's face was red, and his massive hands clenched into deadly fists. "I am going to destroy them!"

Joshua allowed his own rage to boil up. "Stand in line."

Darla stared at Joshua in surprise. He did not care what she was thinking. He stared past her and continued, "Finish your report. I want to know everything about this monster."

Harold looked at Joshua and nodded his head.

Darla cleared her throat and spoke more softly. "I think John was orchestrating a lot of this. Based on the evidence I found, Jerry invested in a lot of the evidence gathered on the senator. John was the brains. I have no doubt he would have eventually turned on Jerry."

Joshua's self-hatred wavered, and a light flooded his shadowy world. *Richard was the man I thought he was. He was like Maria's uncle. Even Harry's correct. These men did kill Richard. They held the gun to his head. They just didn't think Richard would pull the trigger. This wasn't a suicide. This was a conspiracy to murder.*

It felt like the world had come off his shoulders. Then the old feeling of anger returned. *They killed my best friend and caused Barbara's heart attack. John was proud of killing them. They even want to take away what little Harold has left. John is going to pay. I'll make sure of it. Trey and Jerry are scum, but they aren't like John. They've found themselves sucked into John's evil schemes. They should pay for what they've done, but they didn't plot the murders. John is the one I'll see pay for his sins.*

Harold growled his thoughts through his teeth, "Doc, these men are beyond scum. It's too bad you two didn't take them out on the island. We're going to destroy them."

Darla looked at Harold in surprise. "I didn't realize you had a temper."

Harold looked over at her, and his expression began to relax. He responded calmly, "Believe me, I'm controlling it."

Joshua wanted to ask Harold how he was controlling himself, but he was having his own internal battle. Still, his mind and heart fought one another. Deep in his heart, he wanted to kill John, but his brain knew true justice was the better recourse.

Harold turned to Joshua and slapped both hands on the table. "Doc! They were trying to figure out what we knew when they came to the funeral. I bet Richmond is mad because he won't get Dad's company. The blackmail scheme died with Dad, and there is no way the board would even answer his calls after the confrontation Mom and I had with them at the funeral."

Joshua thought about his time with John and his evil friends on the island. "He adjusted his plan after your dad and mom died. John was hoping I could turn the board in his favor. Harry, he had no remorse for what happened. None of it."

Harold sat silently for a moment. Joshua didn't see any signs of him getting angry. His eyes seemed to glaze over. After a minute, he finally spoke.

"Doc, John went after both of us. I know you want John, and so do I. We need to finish this together."

"Harold, I am so sorry you have had to go through all of this." Darla took his hand. "I just wish I could have discovered why John targeted your family."

Harold's whole body appeared to relax at her touch. "Please, call me Harry. I don't really care why. We have the proof they were responsible, and that is good enough for me."

Joshua wanted to know why. Once they had these men in custody, he would ask John. Although it was not ethical, Joshua knew the psychological pressure points to push to get anyone to share information they wanted to hide. But first, they needed to get these men into custody.

"Darla, do you know where the men are now?"

Darla let go of Harold's hand and turned to Joshua. "I do. The senator is back in DC, and both men are back in town at their companies. That's one of the reasons I am being so careful while I'm in the area."

Joshua smiled. "Perfect. We have them exactly where they need to be. Harry, I assume you have your dad's phone book with his political contacts."

Harold smiled and nodded. "I do. Dad worked with a lot of senators on the Armed Services Committee. I know of one senator Dad mentioned at our last party. He's a stand-up guy. I think Dad said he used to fly fighters during Desert Shield. I'm sure he will be interested in this information."

Joshua stood and stretched. He needed to get the tension out of his body. He smiled and sat back down. "I am going to leak this to the press, as well. We think we know whom we can trust, but we can't really be sure. If these men blackmailed Senator Jones and tried to blackmail your father, they certainly are capable of blackmailing others."

Harold took Joshua's cue to relax and stretched his long legs out in front of him. "Good point, Doc. Do you have someone who will take anonymous information?"

Joshua laughed. "Who said I want to be anonymous?"

Darla spoke up. "I guess my work here is done. There's nothing left to do but have lunch and get paid."

Harold smiled. "Would you consider one other assignment?"

Darla slumped in her chair. "As long as it doesn't involve politicians, blackmail, or child molesters."

Harold took her hand into both of his, and Darla sat up again. "Please give me the honor of taking you out to a celebration dinner when this is all over."

Darla attempted to put her other hand around his and smiled. "That is an assignment I'm looking forward to."

Joshua finished off his beer. "If you will excuse me, I'll go check on Maria and lunch."

Harold looked up with a smile. "Take your time, Doc."

Chapter 13

Wednesday morning, Joshua was up at four. He had spent the better part of the afternoon in his home office sending off copies of their documents to local newspapers and television media. Some had called with follow-up questions, and all had said they would pursue the story. Now Joshua reread the blog post he had spent most of the previous evening engrossed in writing. He had apologized to Maria at some point in the night after he shooed her out of his house, but he needed to write this article. His soul demanded it.

Joshua had one sword in his hand, and he was going to make every cut count. He was so determined to complete his piece that he forgot to call Adam and let him know he would be writing the post. At four in the morning, he sent an email to Adam to let him know he was taking the blog back over for the day and cut off Adam's author access. Joshua hoped Adam would not be insulted. Surely, he would understand it was for his protection in case anything in the column caused political blowback. With a warm cup of coffee in his hand, Joshua leaned back to admire and proofread his handiwork.

Readers and colleagues,

I am sure you have heard the news concerning Senator Trey Jones, John Richmond of JR Aerospace, and Jerry Guildford of Guilford Defense Systems. If you are like me, you have many questions. How can men become so full of greed they would try and steal from a family friend? What sort of avarice and narcissism causes men to not only steal from another but to seek the utter destruction of their victims? How did these men become so void of conscience they would even hold their own families in disregard? Why would Senator Jones put his own power and position at risk for the wife and child of his most trusted confidante? Was it only for lust, or did he think he could do anything he wanted simply because he was a US senator?

There are moments in history when all of mankind must acknowledge there is such a thing as evil. A moment when we admit that giving ourselves over to our greed and lust destroys what is good around us. John and Jerry are men who carry more power and have more money than 99 percent of the world, but they want more. Since they could not gain it by competing ethically, they chose a shortcut. A shortcut that has destroyed many families.

The senator gave himself over to his depraved lusts. His actions destroyed his friendship with the Nam family and his closest advisor. Then Senator Jones then went down an even darker path to seduce his friend's daughter. The consequences of his actions gave John and Jerry the power needed to meet their goals.

These sick and twisted people then turned their sights on the Brown family. Their goal was to steal, kill, and destroy. John Richmond's blackmail, based on lies and false evidence, cornered Richard. Being a greedy coward, John could not bring himself to murder Richard outright, so he attempted to buy the company. He assumed Richard was a coward like himself and would simply submit to his blackmail. Because of Richard's integrity, he understood he could not trust John and took the only steps he felt he had left to save his family.

Sincerely,
Dr. Joshua Zeev

Joshua smiled; he wasn't a failure. He was the winner here. John and his cadre would see their plans end this day, and they weren't even aware of it yet. Then his face changed. Conviction hit as quickly as the epiphany.

What have I become? Why am I smiling? I feel happy about this? This isn't good news. This is horrible. It would be less tragic if Richard's death had impacted only the Browns. I'm more concerned with my own reputation and revenge than I am about these people? I'm acting just like John, Jerry, and Trey. He considered deleting his post. *No, I should leave this. What if the press doesn't report the facts correctly? I may need to publish this. It isn't good news, but it is the truth.*

Exhaustion rolled across his whole body, but he would not go back to bed. The blog might need to be posted shortly after the news hit. If he went back to bed, he would not wake up until noon. Joshua walked into the entertainment room and turned on ESPN. He sat down in his recliner and attempted to kill an hour.

"Joshua, wake up. Are you okay?"

Maria gently shook his arm, and Harold hovered nearby.

Joshua covered his mouth and yawned. He rubbed his face, attempted to focus, and spoke. "What time is it?"

"Easy, Doc. It's nine o'clock. Did you sleep at all last night?"

Joshua sat up the recliner. "A little bit. I got up early to proofread my blog. I guess I fell asleep. I need to get up and take care of that."

"Hang on a minute."

Harold reached across and grabbed the TV remote. He flipped to Fox News while Joshua still worked on waking up. *Breaking News* flashed across the television screen. Senator Trey Jones had been found dead in his office at the Capital with a single gunshot wound to his head. An anonymous source reported it a suicide.

"I can guarantee you it's a suicide," Harold said. "I got a call from our congresswoman before we walked over. Congratulations, Doc. We did it!"

Joshua stood up and hugged Harold and then Maria. "Yes, we did!"

Joshua sat back down on the loveseat cattycorner to the recliner. Maria sat down with him.

Harold looked down at Joshua and asked, "Have you posted your blog, Doc?"

Joshua shook his head. "No. I don't think I'm going to."

"Why not? You seemed pretty determined yesterday."

Joshua lowered his head. "I realized early this morning I was becoming just like them. I wanted revenge, not just to see justice done. I will post it only if the news gets the story wrong. From the sound of it, I don't think I need to do that."

Maria turned to Joshua. "The phone keeps ringing and ringing. Harold finally let me take it off the hook."

Harold chuckled. "Yep, and I shut off my cell. I guess nobody can find your number."

Joshua pointed his index finger at his head. "I keep it well concealed. One of the tricks of my trade."

Harold stood. "Mind if I read what you wrote, Doc?"

"Be my guest. The article is already up on my laptop in my office."

Harold left to go read. Maria gave Joshua a big hug. "I'm so proud of you. I knew you were a good man. Richard and Barbara would be proud of you too. You have taken loving care of Harold through all of this."

She released her embrace, and Joshua held her gaze. "I'm not so sure. I came awfully close to crossing the same line as John. I let my self-pity and anger control my motivation. Maybe I looked like I was doing everything right, but given the chance, I could have crossed the line. Speaking of which, what do you think, Maria? Should I still post the blog?"

"If it will help Richard and bring justice, yes."

"Okay, let me see what Harold thinks."

Harold emerged from his reading a brief time later.

"Doc, I need you to post that. People need to know Dad didn't choose to kill himself. They need to hear it from someone who is professionally trained. If I say it, they will think I'm just protecting my father's legacy. I noticed the local news this morning was already questioning some of Dad's role."

Joshua stood and grabbed the television remote. He started flipping through channels to see what other news channels were reporting. CNN had a man claiming to be an expert on national defense speaking with John Berman. They all quieted to hear what the man was saying.

"You see, John, Parabolic Defense Systems could have been in somewhat of a gray area. It isn't unusual for any company to push the limits. Richard Brown was a very successful and shrewd businessman. I hate to speak ill of the dead, but something drove these three men to do these evil acts. After all, people are naturally good inside, and the people in these industries all just want to protect us."

An audible low rumble came from Harold. His hands became large clubs that gripped and squeezed until his knuckles began to pop loudly.

Without breaking his deadly stare at the television, he growled, "Post the article, Doc. Now!"

Joshua and Maria both stood up. "Okay. If you will excuse us for a moment."

Joshua went into the office, proofread his post once more, and published it. "God, let some good come out of all this evil."

Maria came in and put her arms around his neck. "Joshua, God has already answered your prayer."

Joshua stood from his chair, turned, and put his arms around Maria. "Please tell me what God has done."

"Look at Harold. There are men who consider themselves normal but could not have handled what he has been through. How many men could go through what he has and be stronger for it? And you have been here for him. You didn't think you were helping, but you were."

Joshua nodded his head slightly. "I suppose so, but it was such a high price."

Maria tightened her grip around Joshua. "Yes, it was, but God has also brought out the good in you."

"Yes, he has."

Joshua kissed her. Maria giggled a little.

She playfully smacked his shoulder. "No, silly. I mean you have learned to forgive your enemies. You said yourself, your own anger and bitterness were ready to push you over the line. But instead of hating, you chose to forgive them and seek justice. This sets you free and helps protect future victims."

"I suppose so. I just hope my dark days are behind me."

Maria looked Joshua deep in the eyes. "Do you think Harold is against us being together?"

"No, I'm not," Harold said, laughing from the doorway.

Joshua looked up from Maria's eyes with a smile. "I believe you were eavesdropping, Harry."

"I couldn't help it, Doc. I was hoping to pick up some tips to use on Darla."

All three laughed. Maria and Joshua finally released one another.

Harold leaned against the open door. "Actually, I came in to see if Maria could make brunch and if you would join me at my home. I thought the three of us could enjoy a delicious meal out on the deck."

"How about I come over with Maria and help out with the cooking instead?"

"That's fine, Doc. I need to check in with the office. I'm sure they've been trying to call me. I can't stay off the grid for too long."

Chapter 14

The kitchen smelled of beef, bacon, spices, waffles, and eggs. Joshua and Maria had managed to cover the granite island and kitchen counters in flour, mixing pots, and pans with marinade, along with prepped and soon-to-be-plated food. The indigo blue cabinets held a fine layer of white powder, and the mahogany island had drips of dough and powder running down its wood.

Joshua had never had so much fun cooking. Maria's knife skills were seductive and quite dangerous. He needed to make sure never to argue in the kitchen. Cinnamon waffles, eggs, and steak were on the menu. Maria requested Joshua go down into the wine cellar and find them a good wine to go with brunch. He scanned the dozens of old wooden racks nestled up against the cool stone walls. He found a nice Merlot from Sonoma's Rhinefarm Vineyard. Joshua stood at the foot of the stairs when the doorbell rang. A thought popped into his mind. *Reporters. I hope Maria doesn't let them in to find us celebrating.*

Coming out into the kitchen, he put the bottle on the counter. Finding Maria missing, Joshua spoke aloud to himself. "I should go and see if Maria needs help with the press."

Turning around, he found Maria standing next to the kitchen table with a look of terror on her face. Behind her stood John Richmond. As John walked around, the large pistol that John pointed at Maria came into view.

John scoffed. "Well, there he is. Dr. Know-it-all. So glad you came back home to get everything worked out." Then he growled, "Do you know what you cost me?"

Joshua anger overrode any fear John was trying to create. "Do you know what you cost this family?"

He took two steps toward John.

John pointed his pistol at Maria's head. "Easy, Doc. You'd hate to get the help killed. Who would clean up the mess? Did you think you could do this and get away with it? You didn't think I would be coming for you?"

John pointed his gun toward Joshua. Its barrel shook with John's rage. He returned the gun to Maria's head.

"I just got a call from my lawyer. The FBI wants to talk with me. It seems Jerry Boy is already throwing me under the bus. Speaking of buses, where is Harold? I might as well finish what I started. They can only tie me to the gurney once."

Joshua thought he might be able to talk John down. "John, is this all worth it? So far they only have you on blackmail."

John smirked. "Let's not forget murder, Doctor. Everyone is saying it was a conspiracy."

Joshua thought about his blog and prayed John hand not seen it. "Maybe, but that's hard to prove in a court of law. What were your reasons again? You don't need more money. I doubt any jury would find you that greedy. After all, why would you want more? You're already a rich man."

The barrel of John's gun almost bounced with his fury. His voice rose and filled the room. "Rich! You think I'm rich? Look around you, Doctor. This is rich. I merely got the crumbs off Richard's success. A success that would have never happened if we had not started off working together when we first came to this godforsaken town. I'm going down, but I am taking everything that Richard loved with me."

Joshua knew they were all dead if he did nothing but talk. John liked being in control. He expected people to submit to his leverage. Joshua started to walk toward him.

"Are you stupid, Doctor? Do you want this woman's blood on your hands?"

Joshua paused and then spoke evenly, "Her death isn't on my hands. It's on yours. You have the gun. You would pull the trigger. Her life is in your hands, not mine."

He began to slowly walk toward John again.

"Fine!"

John flung Maria to the side, and she slammed into the island counter. Her body crumbled to the floor. John held his shaking gun at Joshua.

Joshua walked up until the barrel pressed against his chest. "Why haven't you fired, John? Of course, right now it's blackmail and money laundering. Legally they can't tie you to the suicide. You pull that trigger, and you'll feel the needle entering your arm. You know it, and I know it."

John pulled back the pistol. "You're right. I can't shoot you. First."

John swung the gun toward Maria's limp body, and Joshua lunged. The gun fired, and the bullet whizzed above Maria's head, embedding in the cabinet. The gun bounced out of John's hand when he crashed to the floor with Joshua on top of him. Joshua slugged John in the head, again and again.

John raised his legs, gripping Joshua by the neck with one leg and under his shoulder with the other. Joshua's back and head slammed against the tile. His world spun momentarily, and he struggled to breathe. John had him in a scissor. Joshua could feel his shoulder slowly cracking and groaning its way out of its joint. Nausea passed up his tight throat, and he gasped for air. His firm neck fought against John's other leg but was no match. His muscles burned, and his airway thinned against John's muscular legs. The room began to dim.

Nobody heard Harold. The roar may have started from his office, but it seemed to come from everywhere and go on forever. Joshua felt his fading body lifted off the ground and then hit with a thud. The scene before him rushed into his restoring vision. He could see Harold had John by the head. Joshua scooted away on his elbows, back over to Maria who now cowered against the cabinets.

Joshua gasped, "Quick, take the path up and around to the front."

Maria grabbed Joshua's shirt. "What about you?"

Joshua looked into Maria's worried eyes. "I need to make sure Harry is okay."

Maria buried her head into Joshua's chest for only a moment then said, "Please be careful."

Joshua smiled and winced. "I'll be okay. Please go."

Maria scrambled to her feet and sprinted for the family room and out the back door. Joshua could hear crunching, and he turned his attention back in the direction of the men. Harold's foot crushed down on John's neck. Richmond's head flopped to one side, grotesquely facing the wrong direction. Harold was twisting John's arm around to tear it from the body.

Joshua drew in a painful breath. "Harry! It's Joshua. It's okay. He's dead. You did it. You saved us. You don't have to tear him apart."

Harold looked at Joshua. His eyes looked dead with no soul or spirit behind them, only blackness. Every blood vessel expanded in the sclera and turned his eyes from white to blood red. Death glared into Joshua's soul. John's gunplay earlier felt like a humorous memory compared to the terror before him. Every fiber of his being wanted to run, but instead he forced himself to sit up. He reminded himself that Harold needed him.

Harold roared once more. Spittle and sweat flung from his lips. His red locks stuck to his face. He looked more like a homeless madman than a future CEO.

"Harry, we're safe. We're okay. You can relax."

Harold noticed the gun lying near John's body. He reached down and grabbed it. Joshua held his breath. Harold wrapped his massive hand around the weapon, and with all his might, slammed the barrel into John's temple. The gun did not travel far, but it went far enough. It stuck out of his head like a macabre work of art. Harold took two steps back and fell on his butt. His breathing started to slow and then became heavier. Drool hit the floor as he struggled to take in more oxygen.

Joshua sat silently until his breathing stilled. Slowly, he made his way to his feet. The pain from his shoulder and neck took his breath away. Joshua slowly walked over to Harold and dropped to his knees. He kissed the top of his head.

"Harry, are you going to be okay?"

Harold nodded. The familiar voice of the young man that Joshua had known for so many years spoke, "Yeah. I'll be okay."

Joshua patted his shoulder. "Are you sure? I don't just mean because you went berserk. You just killed a man."

Harold looked up into Joshua's eyes. There was a stillness there that belied the previous rage.

"You know, Doc, it's kind of weird. I thought I would be more upset. I never wanted to kill anyone, but I don't feel a thing. Does that mean I'm a monster, or is it because it was John?"

Harold started to cry. Joshua sat down and cradled Harold's large body against his. Tears streamed down Joshua's face, as well.

"We'll be okay, Harry."

Maria quietly peeked around the doorframe. She covered her mouth in shock when she saw John's body. Looking at Joshua and Harold, she rushed over, put her arms around Harold, and grabbed Joshua's arms. The three wept together.

Chapter 15

Police descended on the estate. A policewoman and Detective Rodriguez were in the entertainment room questioning Harold at the bar. A CSI team took photos of the bloody pool sitting on the Spanish tile in the kitchen under John's head. Joshua was thankful they had turned off the stove and oven before the police arrived. As soon as the first officers walked into the home, they partitioned everyone away from each other and the crime scene. Fortunately, he stood in the family room with a clear view into the kitchen. He wasn't sure what room they had taken Maria to, but he assumed she was nearby.

Through the kitchen window, he saw a black SUV slide to a stop. The driver had managed to squeeze his vehicle past the police cruiser blocking the driveway entrance and the CSI van blocking the front gate to the plaza. Joshua watched a single man emerge from the large vehicle. His black suit, narrow dark tie, and sunglasses appeared typical of a federal agent. Detective Sanchez was too busy in the family room trying to figure out possible angles and theories about what happened in the kitchen to notice the new arrival.

The man in the dark suit surfaced a brief time later and asked, "Which one of you is Dr. Zeev?"

Sanchez pointed at Joshua, and Joshua smiled and pointed at himself.

The mysterious agent smirked. "That's what I thought. Detective Sanchez, I believe."

The detective stopped, looking down his arm at the bullet in the kitchen cabinet and turned to the agent. "I'm impressed. What can I do for you?"

The dark-suited man pulled a notepad and pen out of his inner jacket pocket. "You could get your CSI people out of my crime scene."

Sanchez looked annoyed and responded curtly. "Excuse me? This is a local crime."

The agent shook his head and began walking between the two rooms. He waved his arms in a shooing motion to get the CSI personnel out of the area. Looking back over his shoulder, he spoke to Detective Sanchez while he attempted to take control.

"Not now. Mr. Richmond was under investigation for his part in Mr. Brown's death. Did you miss the news this morning?"

Joshua was more amused than concerned at the spectacle of the dueling lawmen.

Sanchez shot back a quick reply. "I saw the news. Who are you again?"

The unknown agent walked back into the family room and stood before Sanchez with his hands on his waist. "I'm Agent Garcia Hernandez, CIA."

That was when Joshua noticed a different sort of badge hanging from Agent Garcia's belt.

Joshua cleared his throat. "Excuse me, Agent Hernandez. Do you have an eye problem?"

Garcia smirked. "Never. I'm twenty-twenty. Why?"

Joshua smiled and pointed at his own eyes. "I was wondering if you would mind removing your glasses, so we can see if your face matches your ID badge."

Garcia shook his head and lowered the tone of his voice. "I'm always forgetting these stupid things."

Garcia removed his sunglasses. Joshua swallowed his laugh.

"Detective, I need to speak with Dr. Zeev alone, please."

"My pleasure. I'll go help get you the evidence we have so far on the crime scene."

The detective smiled and shook his head as he left the room.

Agent Garcia pretended not to notice and turned his attention to Joshua. "Dr. Zeev, I am hoping you can help me understand why a suspect in a national security case has his head facing the wrong direction with a gun sticking out of it."

"I didn't do it."

Joshua knew his humor was ill-timed, but he needed to distract himself from the earlier horror.

Garcia laughed. "No, Doctor, I don't believe you did. No offense, but I would be shocked if you had. Let's talk about the elephant in the room, or in the other room—Harold."

Joshua walked over and sat on the leather couch. If this took a while, he was going to be comfortable.

"My statement is the same as I gave the police. John entered the house holding Maria hostage. He held us both at gunpoint. I attempted to disarm John, but he got the better of me. Harold then entered the room. Harold wrestled with John, and I got Maria out of the room. When I turned back, John was as you see him. Harold's a big man. I'm guessing John must have fallen on the gun at some point."

Garcia leaned up against the carved wooden mantel above the large fireplace. "Really? The gun is in the wrong side of his head. Let's not even bring up the fact that his head's pointed the wrong direction. So, I'll make this easy for you. We know about Harold's…um, special ability."

Joshua voiced his surprise before he could stop himself. "How?"

Garcia sat next to Joshua and looked him in the eye. "Doctor, Parabolic was involved in everything from anti-tank weaponry to nuclear missiles. We know exactly where Richard itched and how he scratched himself. I can even tell you where Harold would take his dates after dinner as a teenager. I also know your role in this, but we aren't here to investigate. We already know it was self-defense. We're here to clean things up. I like your story. Stick to it. Our boys will make the photos match. I'm going to brief Harold in a minute."

Joshua let out a sigh. "Thank goodness. I wasn't sure I could lie to the CIA. It really was self-defense. I'm not covering up a murder."

Garcia slapped Joshua on the back of his shoulder. "We know, Doc. Don't worry about a thing. You guys are all good."

The agent shook his hand and stood up. "It's a pleasure to finally speak with you face to face. Don't say anything to Harold, but I'm sure the board will eventually approve him for CEO. Oh, and congratulations on your upcoming wedding."

Joshua stood, alarmed for a moment. "What wedding?"

Garcia laughed. "Doctor, please. I'm CIA. Also, I've been married for twenty-five years. We've had this house under close surveillance ever since Richard's death. Parabolic is a matter of national security, and by extension, so are all of you. We weren't sure what was going on, and we were concerned for the family's safety. We also kept Darla under surveillance. As you know, she's 'retired.' Once you all figured out the case and the police moved in, we assumed we could pull back. It looks like we were a little early on that. Sorry."

Joshua shook his head and stood up. "I guess that should make me feel better, but I'm not sure. How closely have you kept tabs on us?"

"I've seen the way you and Maria look at each other in the photos we've taken. Here's my card. Send me an invite to the bachelor party."

Joshua responded with a touch of sarcasm. "Anything else?"

"If you hear from Jerry Guildford, call me. He was working on a deal, but with John dead, the DA may change her mind. Right now, he's out on bail. I don't know if John's death will change any of Jerry's plans. We want to be careful though. If you so much as see Jerry from across the grocery store, you call me."

Joshua looked down and quickly memorized the phone number on the card. "I promise. Believe me, I don't want any more uninvited guests."

"Good man. Now, let me go find our hero."

Garcia put his sunglasses on and started to leave.

"Excuse me, Agent Garcia, do you need directions?"

"Please. CIA, remember? I've been here before."

With that, Garcia headed out of the room and toward Harold's location. Joshua found his bravado a little over the top but somehow comforting. Joshua meandered into the kitchen and watched CSI finish picking up their equipment. At the top of the driveway sat two more black SUVs. Things were going to get busy again really soon.

From the other side of the kitchen wall, Joshua could hear Harold and Garcia laughing together. Joshua turned and walked outside. He sat down on the sundeck facing the flowing hills, blue sky, and ocean. They had survived.

A wave of grief finally made its way from its hiding spot in Joshua's heart. He bowed his head, and tears began to flow. Salty drops ran off his face, passed the webbing in the sun chair, and fell onto the concrete below. Amidst the anguish, peace finally began to take its hold.

Like an angel from heaven, Maria appeared in the doorway. She did not speak a word. Maria walked over and sat down next to him. She pulled his sobs close to her breast. Joshua felt safe. He could not explain it, and he had no desire to focus on why he was at peace. His tears fell freely from his cheeks to Maria. She draped her long black hair across his face and stroked his cheek with the back of her fingers.

The sun wrapped them both in its warmth, and the cool ocean breeze kept them from becoming too hot. Joshua thought about Richard and Barbara. He felt their presence in that moment. Both spoke to Joshua about Maria. All his worries about their relationship vanished.

Chapter 16

A MONTH LATER, JOSHUA SAT on his front porch. His favorite wooden rocking chair creaked as it rolled back and forth. He enjoyed the first stages of sunset as the orange fireball prepared to sink into the blue Pacific Ocean. The last of the construction trucks were leaving the estate across the street. He could make out Harold's huge silhouette walking up the path toward his house. Maria's shadow looked like a little girl following her father. Harold was counting the days until Darla's return. Their dinner had gone well enough, but then she disappeared on an assignment. All she would tell Harold was not to contact her for eight weeks. The three spent their evenings counting down the days together.

"Hey, Doc! One more week and the office will be completed."

Maria chimed in, "The guest room is very nice, but it has been empty for too long. When will we have guests for the guest room?"

Harold leaned up against one of the posts evenly spaced out on the large front porch as he stared out at the water. "Glad you asked. I want to have Mom's memorial service when Darla returns. I'm going to need all the bedrooms for family. Joshua, do you have any space we can use? I'd like to have as many people here as possible. We're overdue for a party, and I know Mom would want it that way."

Joshua stopped rocking. "That's a great idea, Harry. I can pile as many in my home as we need."

"Perfect," said Harold.

Joshua could see the bags under Harold's eyes were darker and larger than when he saw him for breakfast the previous day.

"Harry, are the dreams any better?"

Harold sat down in the only oversized rocking chair that would hold him. It groaned in protest when Harold began to rock.

"It depends what you mean by "better," Doc. If you mean am I still having them every night, the answer is yes. If you mean are they still making me wake up screaming, the answer is yes."

Maria sat in the chair closest to Joshua. "I agree. Harold scares me some nights. I think he is in trouble."

Joshua got up and dragged his chair next to Harold's. "You know, I can get you medication so you can sleep. It isn't healthy not to sleep."

Harold shook his head. "No, Doc. It's like you've told me for the past month, I have to give my brain time to process that I killed a man."

Joshua grabbed Harold's hand. "You didn't just kill a man. You saved all our lives. You need to remember that."

Harold sighed. "What I need is a good night's sleep."

Joshua released Harold's hand and gave it a friendly pat. "I believe I have something we could all use, and you don't even need a prescription. Is anyone up for some beer?"

Maria raised her hand. "Count me in."

Harold slapped the armrest. "Make that unanimous, Doc."

Joshua opened the screen door. "Be right back."

Maria and Harold began chatting about the memorial service. Inside the kitchen, Joshua pulled out Garcia's card. *I can't believe I'm doing this. I don't really know the man, but he seems to know all of us. There is something about that guy. If nothing else, he will be incredibly entertaining. I hate to put the cart before the horse, but I've learned a few things now. Tomorrow is never guaranteed. As soon as Maria says yes, we are getting married.*

Joshua started his text. *Agent Garcia, would you like to come to my bachelor party? I'll give you the details as soon as I can find a proper engagement ring and Maria says yes.*

Joshua put his phone in his pocket, grabbed the beers from the refrigerator, and headed back out.

Harold took his beer. "Joshua, Maria thinks I should have a mariachi band, but I want a quartet."

Joshua sat down in the rocking chair between Harold and Maria. "Your mother liked a good mariachi band."

Harold chuckled, took a sip of beer, and shot Joshua a sideways glance. "Doc, you're killing me here."

Joshua's phone began vibrating. The message appeared on the locked screen. *Love to, Doctor. I know a guy that can get you the best deals on rings.*

Joshua texted back, *Really?*

A moment later, a reply popped up. *Doctor, please.*

Joshua began laughing. He slid the phone back into his pocket. Harold looked at Joshua confused.

"Doc, what's so funny?"

Joshua attempted to compose himself. "I need to see a man about a horse."

Harold slapped the rocking chair arm and started to laugh.

"Mazel tov!"

Maria looked confused. "Why are you so happy about a horse? Joshua, why are you buying a horse?"

Both men doubled over in laughter.

Maria shook her head. "Boys."

Epilogue

HAROLD SLOWLY STARTED TO WAKE. His fuzzy mind and eyes began to clear and adjust to the light in the master bedroom. The shadow of a man standing over him became clearer. John's familiar bloody face smiled grotesquely in Harold's vision. Despite his small size, he was able to easily pin Harold to his bed.

John spoke with a gurgle and a rasp, "What's the matter, big boy? Afraid? Did you really think killing me could stop me? Hell, I'm here in your house, your parents' master bedroom, and you can't lift a finger against me. Wait and see. I'm still going to win. I've taken over this oversized shack you call home. Next, your business will fall, and you will be nobody. You and Dr. Know-it-all will be nothing but wasted husks."

Harold pushed and pulled but couldn't move. He tried to talk to himself. *Come on, Harry, this is just a dream. Doc told you it was. Don't let your imagination get the best of you. All you have to do is wake up.*

A guttural voice spoke up again. "Come on, Harry, do you really think Doc is right? I'm here. Where is he? He doesn't even believe I exist. Here, let me show you what I'm talking about."

John's head began to snap and pop. He slowly rotated his putrid, fleshy face completely around in a 360-degree turn.

John cackled. "Take that, Linda Blair."

The gun in the side of John's head fell out and landed on Harold's stomach. A drop of blood fell onto his hand.

Harold screamed and roared. He pushed himself up for all he was worth. The light and phantom faded until he saw only his dark bedroom. The shadowy outlines gave way as his eyes adjusted. He was in his new king-size bed in his parents' old master bedroom. He could make out their large antique dresser, which sprawled along the wall across from the bed. The clock on the nightstand read 3:00 a.m. Harold reached over and turned on the night lamp. His silk sheets and comforter sat jumbled and knotted where he had been flailing in his sleep. Then he felt it—a bit of moisture on the top of his hand.

Harold slowly raised it. A drop of liquid trailed across the back of his hand. Harold wasn't sure what it was.

A timid knock at the door made Harold jump. Maria peeked in, and the hall light invaded Harold's dark bedroom.

"Harold, are you okay? Would you like me to call Joshua and get some coffee started?"

Harold ran his fingers through this tangled ginger hair. He looked down at the Spanish tile for a moment while he considered his options.

"Go ahead, Maria. I'm sorry to put you all through this. You both have a lot going on, as well—like wedding plans."

Maria smiled. "Harold, we both love you."

She closed his door, and he could hear her walking down the hall toward the kitchen. Harold knew there was no use in trying to sleep anymore—at least, not before daylight. He got up, stretched, and headed toward the shower. It was going to be another long day.

COMING SOON

HAROLD AND THE ANGEL OF DEATH

BOOK 2
THE BERSERKER SERIES

CPSIA information can be obtained
at www.ICGtesting.com
Printed in the USA
BVHW04s1912300918
528889BV00004B/7/P